THE EDGE OF RUIN

THE EDGE OF RUIN

IRENE FLEMING

THORNDIKE
CHIVERS

This Large Print edition is published by Thorndike Press, Waterville, Maine, USA and by AudioGO Ltd, Bath, England.
Thorndike Press, a part of Gale, Cengage Learning.
Copyright © 2010 by Kathleen Dunn.
The moral right of the author has been asserted.

LIBRARY OF CONGRESS CATALOGING-IN-PUBLICATION DATA

Fleming, Irene, 1939–
　　The edge of ruin / by Irene Fleming.
　　　　p. cm. — (Thorndike Press large print mystery)
　　ISBN-13: 978-1-4104-2877-6
　　ISBN-10: 1-4104-2877-X
　　1. Married people—Fiction. 2. Women motion picture producers and directors—Fiction. 3. Motion pictures—Production and direction—Fiction. 4. New York—History—1898–1951—Fiction. 5. Large type books. I. Title.
PS3557.A414E34 2010b
813'.54—dc22　　　　　　　　　　　　　　　　　　2010015364

BRITISH LIBRARY CATALOGUING-IN-PUBLICATION DATA AVAILABLE
Published in 2010 in the U.S. by arrangement with St. Martin's Press, LLC.
Published in 2010 in the U.K. by arrangement with St. Martin's Press.

U.K. Hardcover: 978 1 408 49199 7 (Chivers Large Print)
U.K. Softcover: 978 1 408 49200 0 (Camden Large Print)

Printed and bound in Great Britain by the MPG Books Group
1 2 3 4 5 6 7 14 13 12 11 10

For Ray Roberts, my very first editor

ACKNOWLEDGMENTS

To all my friends who read this novel early on and helped me plug up the plot holes — Jim Clare, Lee Parks, Annie Stewart, and the incomparable Harold Dunn — thanks. Thanks to the scholars whose interest in early movies moved me to write it. You can find a bibliography of their work on my Web site, www.irenefleming.com. Also thanks to Charles Salzberg and Michael Neff at Algonkian, who bucked me up when I needed confidence. But, mostly, thanks to Peter Rubie, my agent, to Janet Hutchings, who introduced me to him, to Keith Kahla, my editor, and to all the helpful souls at Minotaur.

ONE

One sunny afternoon in the fall of 1909, Adam Weiss came home to the three-story Dutch Colonial house he shared with his new wife in suburban Philadelphia, hung his derby hat on the hat rack, and announced to her that he was selling his string of nickelodeons — and everything else the couple owned — to go to New York City and set himself up as a movie producer. Emily was stunned. It was as if he had said, "Hello, sweetheart, I'm home, now say good-bye to the crystal chandelier, the oriental carpets, the mahogany furniture we bought only three months ago, say good-bye to your cook and your maid. We're going into the movie business."

Emily gazed around the parlor at these beloved objects (all except the cook and the maid, who were at work in the kitchen), and then up at her husband's face, seeking some overt sign of insanity in those beautiful hazel eyes, some telltale quiver of madness in that silky dark mustache. Last week they had celebrated his twenty-ninth birthday. She had heard of men losing their minds as they approached the age of thirty.

She was not reassured by Adam's insistence that he had what it took — expertise, professional connections — to succeed as a producer. "I've been an exhibitor for so long that I think it's time for me to move on, try something new. Distribution doesn't interest me, but the opportunities in production are enormous." He paced the floor, trembling with excitement.

"Are you in some kind of trouble, Adam?"

"Nothing you could call trouble. A small problem with Thomas Edison and his Motion Picture Patents Company."

"You didn't pay the Trust this week?"

"Of course I paid them. Two dollars a week to Mr. Edison's Trust for every one of my theaters. If I didn't pay I couldn't show Patents Company licensed movies. But you know what? I'm tired of it. It's a protection racket. I'm not paying them next week, or ever again. Good-bye, Mr. Edison." He touched the fingers of one hand to his forehead and snapped them outward in a farewell salute. There was an unusual brightness in his eye, surely a sign of something abnormal.

"Just like that," she said. Why had she left a paying job in the chorus to marry this man? It was true that she was not a huge success as a chorine, being too slim and lacking in bosom, but everyone had admired her luxuriant auburn hair.

"Yep, just like that." Adam lit up a Lucky Strike and began to wave it around. "I'm not alone in this, you know. Movie men all over the country are going independent. In Chicago, there's a whole —"

"But why get into production?"

"The independent distributors need product."

"Product?"

"Movies to rent out to the exhibitors."

"Ah."

"Dramas. Comedies. Audiences want to see a new movie every night, and a story movie, too, not a travelogue or a replay of the coronation of King Edward. You wouldn't believe the income potential in making these things. To say nothing of the creative opportunities." He tapped his cigarette, sending the ashes into the rubber plant. "Of course I'll need your help, as an experienced show person."

"So when you make these movies, you

have an outlet all lined up for distributing them?"

"I'll tell the world I have." He opened his briefcase and handed her a copy of a contract he had signed with someone named Howard Kazanow. Emily spread it out on the Queen Anne tea table — one of the things Adam meant to sell, along with the rugs, the silver, the rest of the furniture, the brand-new Locomobile, even Emily's own beloved mink coat — and read it through twice.

The contract was terrifying. It required Adam's movie company to deliver four one-reel movies by the twenty-third of the month: two Westerns, a comedy, and a drama. If they failed, Mr. Kazanow took the whole movie company, which meant everything they owned, since Adam was proposing to sell it all to finance the company. "Did you show this to a lawyer, by any chance?"

"Howie Kazanow is a lawyer," Adam said. "He's a very smart businessman, Emily. I knew him in college." Completely mad, Emily thought. Mother was right. I should have waited longer before I married him. There was plenty of time. I'm only twenty-five. I could have stayed in the chorus of the touring company of *Monkey Days* and gone on with the others to Chicago.

He threw his cigarette on the carpet and ground it underfoot. "Don't look at me like that. I have to do this, sweetheart. Later on we'll have kids, responsibilities. I'll be stuck in Philadelphia forever."

"But, Adam. All our money."

"Don't worry," he said. "Next month I'll cover you with diamonds. Look at this." He produced a cardboard box and opened it to reveal, not diamonds, but a ream of snowy stationery bearing a letterhead in the very most modern typeface. "What do you think of this? Rag paper, twenty-pound bond."

"Melpomeen," she read. "Melpomeen Moving Picture Studios." In the middle of the *M* was an elegant curlicue.

"No, sweetheart, Mel*pom*ene. It rhymes with hominy."

"Who's going to know that?"

"Anyone with a classical education. Melpomene is the muse of tragic drama." So it was to be a tragically dramatic enterprise, somehow making use of Adam's two years of college.

"There's no street address."

"I bought a typewriter last week, sweetheart. As soon as we get our money we'll build a studio with a real street address, and whenever we need to write letters you can type it in."

Insane. But how good-looking he was. How she loved the cleft in his chin, his noble chin that made him look like those tall, handsome young millionaires in the drawings of Charles Dana Gibson. "Is it truly possible to make four movies in three weeks?"

"People do it all the time," he said. "With an indoor studio and arc lights, they make four movies every week. You and I can do that, too, Emily. Melpomene is your business as much as mine. We're as smart as any of those guys making movies in New York." She had never seen him so wildly happy, even on their wedding night.

And so she swallowed her misgivings and agreed to become a partner in this mad enterprise, to write scenarios, hire actors, sew costumes, do the lettering for the inter-titles, and design Melpomene's trademark M that was to appear in every shot.

It took a week for them to dispose of their property in Philadelphia, from discharging the cook, the maid, the chauffeur, and Adam's valet through finding buyers for the house and the car to watching the workmen roll up the parlor rug and march out the front door carrying it on their shoulders, the last of the Weisses' possessions. The last, that is, if you didn't count Adam's extensive wardrobe. For although Adam insisted that Emily must sell her fur coat, which he gave her before they were married, he himself refused to part with so much as a silk hat.

At Grand Central Depot in Manhattan, while Adam arranged for transportation to the hotel, Emily bought some magazines and sat down on a wooden bench, polished by many rumps, to catch up on her reading. Somehow she felt that a return to life in New York City would be easier to face if she had full knowledge of all the new trends. A sour cloud of stale cigar smoke washed over her.

She buried her head in the latest copy of *McClure's.* The magazine was full of stories of labor unrest, capital abusing labor, labor attacking capital, labor and capital banding together to prey on the ordinary citizen. According to *McClure's,* anarchy was on the rise, thanks to the Industrial Workers of the World and other organized tentacles of the Red menace.

But according to *Hampton's,* anarchy was not a danger at all, and, far from bringing down industrial civilization, the IWW was civilization's last great hope. Neither story had it right, in Emily's opinion. She knew about unions; she knew about anarchy. When she was still single and living in New York three of her roommates were garment workers. She used to attend anarchist Emma Goldman's bracing lectures, before the police began closing them down.

It was true that Miss Goldman's exhortations aroused even in her law-abiding Yankee vitals a latent urge to go out and smash the state. From their cheers and clapping she could almost have said that similar feelings were stirring in the corseted breasts of the other women present, leisured uptown women for the most part, since the workingwomen were still in their sweatshops. But what was the end result? When the speeches were over and the lecture hall was dark, very few of those ladies rushed out and became Wobblies of the IWW, or even Democrats. For one thing, as women, they didn't have the vote. Now, *that* would be something to struggle for.

Emily put *McClure's* and *Hamptons* aside with a sigh and picked up *Theatre Magazine*. Aha! Here was a story of how *The Heiress's Cousin* had closed at Belasco's Stuyvesant after three performances. Surely the closing would provide a rich source of unemployed actors (for instance, the leading player, aging matinee idol Robert Montmorency,

"Fast-handed Bob" as the chorines in Philadelphia used to call him). Emily remembered Montmorency, the eyebrows, the little mustache, his acting skills impressive as long as he was sober, some said. Now, if only he were hungry enough to take a job in moving pictures, he might be induced to play villains with the Melpomene company. Emily noted that the theatrical agency handling Montmorency was the same one that had found her the job in the chorus of *Monkey Days.* She would call on them tomorrow, looking stunningly rich and dignified in her gray faille walking suit.

But was it still in fashion? She turned her attention to *The Delineator.* Happily, the magazine was showing a suit not unlike her own in cut and color, as well as a number of lovely frocks designed to be worn without corsets. New Women were discarding their corsets, those steel-boned instruments of torture that mangled the internal organs, and so was Emily, who preferred to wear a bust bodice and drawers under her rational dress. A woman who declined to cripple herself with corsets had the physical strength to support a really good hat.

Emily sighed over the picture of an embroidered chiffon tea gown, wispy, flowing, tight only in the bosom. Such gowns were made to be worn at home. When Adam provided her with a home again, if that day ever came, she would have one made up in the palest lavender and invite someone over for tea.

She tucked the magazines into her bag, waved away another cloud of cigar smoke, and straightened her really good hat. Here came Adam with a porter.

At 1466 Broadway, right on the new subway line and a short walk from the major theatrical agents and suppliers, the Knickerbocker was the hotel of choice for affluent show folks. Adam told the desk clerk they wanted a room with a private bath. The bath was for developing film, he whispered to Emily on the elevator, when she complained about the expense. The bellhop showed them to a lovely room on the eleventh floor, with yellow-figured wallpaper, handsome woodwork, high ceilings, and a shiny, ornate brass bed. Emily sat on it, trying the springs, while Adam threw up the window sash.

"Look here, darling," he said.

"What?"

He took her hand and drew her to the window. "Manhattan. The world. Soon it will all be ours."

Emily looked out at the building across

the way, the purpling twilit sky beyond it, and then down at the street. Noises drifted up, horse sounds, car horns, shouts, a fire wagon clanging past. Streetlights winked on. She shivered; the air was cold. Adam put his arm around her, held her tight, and made her lean out of the window. "Just look," he said. "Way over there is Delancey Street, where my parents lived. I've come a long way since those days."

She didn't want to look. "Thanks, I've seen it," she said. "I lived in Manhattan once, too, you know." Not only that, but high places made her uncomfortable. The sight of those tiny people and objects moving to and fro, the sight of the hard sidewalk far below her, beckoning. . . . "Let go of me."

"Oh, well, if you feel that way," he said.

"It's cold out there," she said. "And I have to hang these clothes up." She busied herself putting the room in order, turning her back on the view from the high window.

Two

The following morning, while his wife was pinning up her hair and preparing to go see her old casting agent about some suitable actors, Adam Weiss went forth in pursuit of a cameraman. Silent partner Howie Kazanow had given him the street address of a technician by the name of Angus Johnson, who owned his own movie camera and filmed for independent companies sometimes.

The trolley line passed very close to Angus Johnson's house. Adam stepped off the car into a quiet neighborhood. No trees relieved the view of endless brick row houses, endless swaths of wiring swooping from one telephone pole to the next, endless cobblestone streets buried in dirt and horse dung, but at least there was no swarm of tenement dwellers shouting in foreign tongues and reeking of garlic. A tired old horse clopped along, pulling a knife-grinder's wagon, raising a small cloud of dust. The sound of the knife-grinder's bell brought out a woman with a handful of kitchen knives, and the wagon stopped. Her house was next door to Johnson's.

A turn on the crank of the bell summoned a short, fat, scowling person to the door, drying her hands on a flowered apron.

"I've come to see Mr. Johnson," Adam said.

Her scowl deepened. "There's no one by that name here."

"Just a minute," Adam said. He stuck his foot in the door as she tried to close it. "Mr. Howard Kazanow told me I could find Mr. Johnson at this address. I have some work for him."

"That's different," the woman said. "*Angus!* There's a man here wants to hire you to do some work."

A tall man in shirtsleeves, as gaunt and gangly as the woman was squat and pudgy, shuffled into the hall. His big-knuckled hands were marked with burn scars and strange chemical stains. "Who did you say sent you?"

"Howard Kazanow."

"Oh. That's all right then. Thank you, Martha; I'll take care of the gentleman."

"Humph," the woman said, and waddled

into the back part of the house.

Mr. Johnson brushed a hank of long gray hair out of his eyes and squinted at Adam. "What sort of work?"

"I'm filming some pictures. Mr. Kazanow assured me that your camera work was the best."

"Come inside." Adam stepped into the hallway. Mr. Johnson put his head out, looked up and down the street, and quickly shut the door. "When do you want to film your picture?"

"On the first sunny day. Tomorrow or the next day, if possible. Time is of the essence. My plan was to have the actors meet us in the Bronx, by the zoo. It's fairly rural, and we can stage some scenes out behind the —"

"Oh, no," Mr. Johnson said. "Not the Bronx. You can't make movies in the Bronx, not with things the way they are."

"What things?" Adam said.

"Mr. Thomas Edison's studio is in the Bronx. Right by the zoo."

"Surely Mr. Edison and his people will be too busy with their own work to bother with —"

"Did Mr. Kazanow tell you everything?"
"Perhaps not."

"Come into the parlor, Mr. Weiss. Sit

down. Martha! Bring us some tea."

Adam would have preferred whiskey, or even a martini, that astringent new drink that the Italian bartender at the Knickerbocker had introduced him to the night before while Emily was sleeping, but the sun was not yet over the yardarm, wherever the hell that was; in fact it was hardly ten thirty in the morning. He selected a platform rocker with hand-tatted antimacassars from among several other maroon plush chairs in the parlor and accepted a hostile cup of tea from Martha. He took a sip; it was nasty. She must have kept it simmering on the back of the stove for days.

Mr. Johnson sat in silence for a moment, composing his thoughts. At last he spoke. "You know anything about Mr. Edison's Motion Picture Patents Company, Mr. Weiss?"

"Enough, I guess. I owned a string of moving picture theaters in Philadelphia."

"But your production company is not one of Edison's. Is that right?"

"That's right," Adam said. "Melpomene is an independent company. That's the whole point of this endeavor."

"If you're not one of his companies, Mr. Edison will do everything he can to keep you from making movies. He will try to stamp you out. That's what conditions are like right now in the moving picture industry."

"Is that so." Adam lit a cigarette. Had he come all this way, risking everything, only to fall victim to Edison again? No, by God. "I think Mr. Edison will find Melpomene Moving Pictures a little harder to stamp out than he thinks."

"Not if you set up to film in the Bronx, right under his nose, Mr. Weiss. Even at that, you'll find Edison's lawyers and detectives everywhere you go in the city. Or they'll find you. Aside from the lawsuits, his people have been known to break cameras, ruin film, and worse. Some of them are nothing but hooligans."

"But there are independent companies making movies here, aren't there?"

"Yep, there are, but they only last as long as they can keep Mr. Edison's detectives away from their movie cameras."

"What are these detectives looking for?"

"The Latham Loop."

"That bit of slack in the film that lets it slide smoothly through the projector."

"Yes, and through the camera, exposing one frame after another."

"Did Edison invent that?"

"Nope. Latham did. I nearly did it myself,

when I was working at Mr. Edison's laboratory in West Orange. But Mr. Edison keeps control of the patent."

"Clever of him."

"Has to. Make no mistake, Mr. Weiss, Mr. Thomas Alva Edison lives by his patents. If it wasn't for his movie and phonograph patents Mr. Thomas Alva Edison would be stone broke."

"I can't believe that."

"All the same. He lost millions of dollars in the iron ore scheme, every cent he got for the sale of Edison General Electric and a lot more besides. Now he's plowing everything back into his alkaline batteries."

"So what you're telling me is that this is very important to him, crushing my little business." Adam considered asking Johnson about the iron ore scheme and the batteries, but the fact was he didn't care. The important point seemed to be that Mr. Edison was willing to go to great lengths to protect his own interests. Understandable, but damned inconvenient. "Tell me this, though. How do the other independent movie companies get around the problem of the Trust?"

"They work on the outskirts of the city. They sneak around. Sometimes they hide their real camera in a milk wagon or a stand of bushes, and pretend to film with another camera without the Edison patented shutter. Of course the fake cameras take terrible pictures. But usually the independents make their movies where Edison's detectives can't find them. Not right out in plain sight in the Bronx."

"I see," Adam said. "Very well, Mr. Johnson, we'll line up another location. I'll let you know where, and you can meet us there. Is there a telephone number where I can reach you?"

Mr. Johnson handed him a piece of paper. "This is the number of the candy store across the street. They'll call me to the telephone, or if I'm not home they'll take a message."

After the phone number Johnson had written a street address. "What's this address?" Adam said.

"A shop where you can buy film. Tell them I sent you; they keep it under the counter."

"I have to use contraband film?"

"Mr. Eastman and Mr. Edison are like that," Johnson said, holding up his chemical-stained hand with the first two fingers crossed tightly together to indicate a close relationship. "Great hunting and fishing pals. Eastman won't sell his film to movie companies who aren't in the Trust. My source smuggles the Lumière film stock over from France."

"I see."

"It's good film, but it's got no sprocket holes. You have to punch them yourself."

"Punch them myself?"

"I guess you can borrow one of my punches," Mr. Johnson said. "Here you go." He handed Adam a naked greasy mechanism, clumsy to hold and heavy.

"Thank you. Er —" Before Adam could demand wrapping paper Mr. Johnson hustled him to the front door.

"We can start tomorrow if the weather is good. Of course, that's up to you. Oh, and you might think about hiring some big, strong fellows in case some of Mr. Edison's boys come around, McCoy or Duffy particularly. Duffy can be pretty unpleasant. But McCoy is the worst." Mr. Johnson opened the front door and glanced up and down the street. No McCoy; no Duffy. Nothing was in sight except a horse-drawn ice wagon slowly passing. "I'll be waiting for your call," Johnson said. "Be sure you aren't followed." SHULTZ'S ICE read the sign on the wagon. Harmless-looking, Adam thought, but you never knew where Edison's secret army of detectives might be lurking.

Adam waited until the menacing ice

wagon was out of sight before he slipped out the door and made for the trolley. No detectives, no persons other than Adam himself, got on at his trolley stop. He went straight to the shop that carried the Lumière film, stopping only to buy a newspaper in which to wrap the borrowed sprocket-hole punch, so as to keep the grease from getting on his good suit.

The shop was a hole-in-the-wall on a busy street at the edge of Greenwich Village, barely visible between a fruit stand and a store selling ladies' hats. As he slipped inside Adam saw a uniformed policeman out of the tail of his eye, slowing down, stopping. He started guiltily, but the policeman had paused only to take a piece of fruit.

A young salesclerk wearing a celluloid collar and cuffs, arm garters, and center-parted hair stood behind the counter. Adam waited until the policeman had moved along, and then he said to the clerk, speaking low, "Angus Johnson sent me."

At the sound of the cameraman's name the clerk laid his forefinger next to his nose. After some further discussion he readily provided twelve thousand feet of film, enough and to spare for shooting and processing the four one-reel movies. Adam paid him and stepped out into the immigrant-crowded street, glancing around to be sure there was not a policeman in sight. There was not.

Melpomene Moving Picture Studios was officially in business.

THREE

That night Emily and Adam dressed for dinner, like the plutocrats they longed to become. Emily had never seen a handsomer man than Adam in evening clothes. She still had her green gown of slipper satin, but no fur coat to wear over it.

"My cloth coat won't look right," she said.

Adam collapsed his opera hat and put it back in the hatbox. "Fear not, my dear. We'll dine in the hotel."

A puff of face powder took the shine off Emily's nose; a simple headdress of rhinestones and ostrich feathers completed the effect. She stood back from the mirror to admire herself. "Won't it be expensive, dinner at the Knickerbocker?"

"Don't worry about it," Adam said. "The tab won't come due until after we fulfill our contract with Howie Kazanow. In a few weeks we'll be rich beyond the dreams of avarice." He looked over her shoulder into the mirror to adjust his tie.

"What if we fail?"

"We can't fail, sweetheart. But if we do" — he kissed her on the ear — "one more debt will be as nothing." Emily imagined the two of them in rags, fleeing their creditors, riding the rods of a boxcar into the West. Perhaps it would be romantic.

A small string orchestra was playing as Emily and Adam swanned into the Knickerbocker dining room. The puffed-up maître d'hôtel led them through ferns and white gleaming tables, past couples less pretty than they were, to the very best table in the house. As they passed, heads turned and the clinking of silverware stopped.

"We'll start with the oysters Rockefeller," Adam told the waiter. "After that, *poularde à la bonne femme . . .*" and he launched into a stream of restaurant French, which Emily knew he had learned at college, waiting on tables to put himself through. Adam's French was about as fluent as the Italian Emily had picked up working in the corps de ballet of various operas. Nevertheless, she had never known him to order a bad meal. ". . . And bring us a bottle of Château Grand Vin Clos de la Garde to start with," he concluded.

The waiter left. Emily asked whether in

all that stream of verbiage Adam had ordered anything for dessert.

"Not yet. So tell me about the actors you engaged."

"I went to my old agency," Emily said. "The one where I used to sit in the outer office day after day waiting for work. I told that awful Rita I was there to hire some people. You should have seen her face."

"Must have been gratifying."

Emily smiled. Gratifying didn't begin to express it. "There were two young Indian fellas waiting to see Mr. Schwartz. Perfectly adorable. Just the thing for the Westerns, I thought, so I told them to —"

"Actors?"

"Adam, we're making movies. They don't have to be actors, they just have to look good."

"Not actors."

"High steelworkers. They just finished the Blackwell's Island Bridge, and they thought they might like to try show business for a change. You should see their posture. Maybe they can do stunts."

"Did you hire any actors, sweetheart?"

"Yes! Robert Montmorency. You must have heard of him. A famous man, Broadway star, Shakespearean actor —"

"My mother admired him," Adam said.

"What's he done lately?"

"*The Heiress's Cousin,* at the Stuyvesant. Not his fault it closed. Before that, I didn't ask. Then there's Vera Zinovia. Beautiful girl, pale skin, dark eyes, masses of raven hair."

"Russian?" The wine steward arrived and began his performance with the wine, uncorking it, offering Adam the stopper to sniff.

"Very Russian," Emily said. "She trained at the Moscow Art Theater."

"Does she speak any English?"

"Enough to take stage directions. Also she knows many expatriate actors who live on the Lower East Side. She promised to introduce me to them. We still have to find a juvenile, and she says she knows some good ones. And after Vera, Fay Winningly."

"I think I remember her. She's been in other movies." The wine steward poured about a tablespoonful of wine into Adam's glass. Adam swirled it around, sniffed it, tasted it, and nodded approval.

"Fay is a very successful movie actress," Emily assured him while he did the business with the wine. "She has a waiflike quality that comes across well on film. Her last job folded up because the producers went bankrupt; some trouble with lawsuits from the Trust, she said. I thought Edison only made trouble for the exhibitors and distributors."

"Edison makes trouble for everyone," Adam said. "Mr. Johnson gave me an earful this morning." The oysters arrived. Adam frowned and busied himself with them.

"What did he say?"

Adam swallowed an oyster and gestured with his cutlery. "Edison has his knife out for the independent producers right now. You know the Kodak film? George Eastman is in bed with the Patents Trust. We have to use smuggled French film. Also we have to watch out for Edison's Trust detectives. They're all over the place, inspecting the cameras, reporting to Edison's lawyers, sometimes even vandalizing movie company property."

"Good heavens."

"Don't worry, sweetheart. We'll beat him. 'Our strength is as the strength of ten because our hearts are pure.' " The waiter whisked the oyster shells away and then the partridge came, followed by the other courses, each more succulent than the last. After the Clos de la Garde Adam ordered a well-chilled bottle of Mumm's Extra Dry. Emily loved champagne; she drank it down with a light heart. And why not? Adam was perfectly correct. Under the circumstances the bill for the dinner was the least of their worries.

"So you haven't hired a juvenile?" Adam said at last. The role of the juvenile was for a handsome, innocent-faced young man to pair up with the lovely Fay Winningly in different scenarios.

The waiter placed her charlotte russe in front of her. Emily took a delicate spoonful. "No one was quite right."

"How could that be?"

"It just was. I must have looked at a hundred head shots. No one was right. They all looked too young, or too old, or too jaded, or too feebleminded. I was ready to go out and cast the first good-looking young man I met on the street. After all, this is the movies. Do we really need a trained actor? But Vera Zinovia told me she knew somebody. She said for us to meet her in Greenwich Village at the Café Boheme on Christopher Street tomorrow evening at eight. She told me many foreign actors congregate there, including her cousin Boris, the finest actor in the northern hemisphere."

"So. Another day before we can start filming."

"We can use the time to round up some costumes and scout out a good location.

Somewhere far from Mr. Edison's detectives. How much trouble is this Patent Trust going to be? We might want to throw in our lot with them, Adam. It might be easier to cooperate with the Wizard of Menlo Park than to try to outwit him. Why wouldn't we want to do that?"

"Other than the fact that the Motion Picture Patents Company is the earthly embodiment of evil, you mean?"

"Surely Mr. Edison can't be that bad. After all, he invented the lightbulb, by whose light we are eating this excellent dinner, he invented the phonograph, everyone says he's a genius —"

"Did you ever see that film where he electrocuted the elephant?"

Emily shuddered. She had.

"He electrocuted that blameless elephant, as well as a number of dogs, and they tell me he even helped design the electric chair, all so that he could get the better of Mr. Westinghouse, a business rival."

"And now in our small way we are going to become his business rivals, too," Emily said. "Don't you think he will try to electrocute us, too, figuratively speaking? Don't you think we should —"

"Even if it were possible for Melpomene to throw in its lot with the Trust," Adam said, "and I think it isn't, not at any price, I can see myself joining them as a producer and then hearing from Mr. Edison that there's not enough moral uplift in my work, or enough electrocuted animals, or enough boxing cats. Remember the boxing cats? I want to make good movies. I want to make Art. If I only wanted to make money I would have stayed in Philadelphia with my string of nickelodeons." He looked very serious, very artistic.

"I love you, Adam," Emily said. He squeezed her silk-clad knee under the table. "We'll keep out of Mr. Edison's way then."

"Sure we will. We'll find a better location than the Bronx. How about Jersey?"

"Menlo Park is *in* Jersey," she said.

"Edison left Menlo Park some time ago, sweetheart, as everybody knows. He's based in West Orange."

"But —"

"I mean someplace like Fort Lee or Coytesville. That's a long way from West Orange. We can take the ferry across the Hudson. The people who sold me the film said there are independent movie companies filming over there already. You couldn't ask for better scenery. They have everything. Woods, fields, rocky cliffs, village streets, attractive storefronts, everything."

Rocky cliffs. Indeed there were, Emily thought, and the Palisades were the rockiest and most clifflike of them all. It was there on a picnic with Ricky Schwartz that she had suffered her first serious episode of height fear, three years and a whole career in show business ago. But Adam didn't have to hear about Ricky, or about Emily's fear of heights, which she had transcended, mostly, the day she wed Adam and became a secure married woman. "Will we use the cliffs in our pictures?"

"We will," he said, "and the storefronts, if we like them, and every interesting scene we can find in the out-of-doors. When these first four pictures are finished and distributed we'll have the money to build our own studio for indoor work. Maybe we'll build it right there in Fort Lee."

Visions of wildly creative moviemaking replaced all thoughts of the terrifying cliff. Emily was beginning to see that Adam was an artist, not a common, ordinary madman at all. She could help him make art. With a lot of luck, she could help him make money, too.

They went up to bed and made steamy love until the hotel room warmed up. In the dark bathroom, with the smell of Adam's sweat still on her skin, Emily punched holes in the raw film stock while Adam lay in bed in his socks and garters writing movie scenarios. This is how it's supposed to be, Emily thought. This is living. She was tremendously excited.

By the time Emily had finished punching holes Adam was snoring, lying on his back with one arm over the top of his head. One more task remained to be done before she could curl up beside him. Every moving picture studio of any consequence had a trademark to keep the unscrupulous from pirating their films, AB for American Biograph, the rooster for Pathé, the flying V for Vitagraph, and so forth. Besides appearing in all the titles, the emblem was displayed in nearly every shot. For scenes filmed indoors in a studio the trademark was painted somewhere on the woodwork or hung on the wall like a picture. For outdoor scenes it was nailed to a tree or stuck in the ground attached to a sharp stake. If you wanted your work to be respected, you had to have a professional-looking emblem. Emily sat down gently on the foot of the bed, took scissors and cardboard, and by the pale orange light of the dressing table lamp cut out the trademark M for Melpomene.

FOUR

The Café Boheme was in a cellar just off Christopher Street, down a short flight of stone steps from the sidewalk. Adam pulled the door open and held it for Emily. She hoisted her skirt a few inches, to keep it from the dry leaves and general filth swirling in the stairwell, and stepped inside.

A steamy smell of coffee, tobacco smoke, unwashed workers, and cheap perfume rolled over her. The large room beyond the door was packed with such a crowd as she had never seen before gathered in one place. Sloe-eyed factory girls from the Lower East Side, exotic, Mediterranean, in cheap and threadbare jackets, were keeping company over cups of coffee with fresh-faced New England boys wearing the school colors of Harvard and Yale knitted in striped six-footer mufflers. Artistic types were huddling over the latest copy of *Camera Work,* the magazine of avant-garde photographs, some

40

of them women, all of them smoking cigarettes. Men in work clothes, a few women
among them, were crowding around the
iron stove in the far corner. Everyone
seemed to be talking at once at the tops of
their lungs. The level of sound was almost
unbearable. Adam said something.

"What?"

Adam spoke louder. "Where is she?"

Emily blinked away tears from the cigarette smoke, looked around the room, and
shrugged. Vera Zinovia was nowhere to be
seen. At the table in front of them a Harvard boy was saying to his stunningly beautiful companion, "What do you mean, you
don't believe in free love? You told me you
were a New Woman."

The people with the photo magazine were
arguing hotly. "But this is against everything
the photo-secessionists stand for. Stieglitz
says —"

"Nonsense. He never said that." The thin
woman sat gracelessly with her knees apart,
showing her petticoat. She poked her cigarette at the pimply young man she was arguing with. So this was bohemia. Emily reflected that she preferred the society of
actors. Their manners were more elegant.
She looked around for Vera and her friends.

A big tall man with one dead eye towered

41

over the mêlée in front of the stove, preaching in a loud voice about labor politics. Emily spotted Vera at last, standing next to him, gazing raptly into his face. Her cheeks were pale, her fiery eyes were ringed with kohl, her lips were like strawberries. Well, not strawberries, strawberries had those little seeds all over them, but they were red and puffy and she made a lovely picture. What a success she would be in the movies.

"Gompers is dead wrong. We have to have a general strike," the big man boomed. "And I'll tell you why."

"This way," Emily said to Adam, making her way among the closely packed tables. "Excuse me." Her heel had got itself tangled in the end of a blue and white college scarf whose other end was still wrapped around the neck of a youth. The young man glanced at her, tugged the scarf free, and returned his attention to his female companion.

Next to the stove a short, plain woman toasted her skirts as the big man was holding forth. Emily recognized Emma Goldman, whose talks used to inspire her so.

"Hear him," Miss Goldman said. "Without solidarity among workingmen and women we will never defeat the capitalists."

"Hell's fire," Adam said. "It's a meeting of the Industrial Workers of the World. I hate unions."

"They're just talking and drinking coffee," Emily said. "After we speak with Vera we can leave. She promised to introduce us to the finest actor in the northern hemisphere."

"Really. He's here, is he? I suppose he's in that crowd of Wobblies."

The big man thundered on. "Some of you remember the first general strike in Coeur d'Alene, when all the mines were closed down to prevent a reduction of wages. First thing the mine owners did was to bring in thugs carrying six-shooters and rifles. There was a pitched battle between miners and thugs. People died." Emily scanned the faces turned toward the big man, wondering which face belonged to the finest actor in the northern hemisphere. Many of the faces were dirty and hairy, but perhaps with a shave, some soap, some greasepaint . . .

Suddenly one face stood out for her, a diamond in a bowl of pebbles. It was an open, honest face, the face of a classic juvenile lead. His lips were perfect, his nose straight and fine, his hair like ripe wheat. Emily took him for a student, until she saw that his hands bore the deeply ingrained grime of hard physical labor; he must be one of these Wobblies.

"Then the mine owners asked the governor for soldiers, and the soldiers came. Who brought the soldiers? Railroads manned by union men; engines fired with coal mined by union men. Our brother workers. After that came the strike in Bitter Wash, which has become a household word in labor circles throughout the world."

The young man looked up suddenly at the name of Bitter Wash, his face illuminated by the flickering light of a candle stuck in a wine bottle. If only it were possible to capture that look on camera. Emily had to have the young man's face in her movies.

"In Bitter Wash, five thousand men went out on strike in sympathy with forty-five workers belonging to the mill men's union in Colorado City. You will recall that those forty-five men were discharged simply because they were trying to improve their standard of living, and replaced with scab mill men by the mine owners, using state troops and the influence of the federal government.

"The workers in Bitter Wash struck in sympathy. After months of hardship, after sixteen hundred of our men had been arrested, after four hundred of them had been loaded aboard special trains guarded by soldiers, shipped away from their homes, dumped out on the prairies of New Mexico

44

and Kansas, after the women who had taken up the work of distributing strike relief had been placed under arrest — the mine owners were able to man the mines with scabs, the mills running with scabs, the railroads conveying the ore from Bitter Wash to Colorado City run by union men — the connecting link of a proposition that was scabby at both ends!" The big man paused and mopped his brow. "We were not thoroughly organized. There has been no time when there has been a general strike in this country." The Wobblies gave out murmurs of assent.

Vera Zinovia squeezed the big man's hand and broke away from the group to come and see Emily. One of the dark men followed her, his walk almost as sinuous as Vera's own. This must be the finest actor in the northern hemisphere.

Sure enough, Vera introduced him as her cousin from the Moscow Art Theater, Boris Ivanovich Levin.

"How do you do, Mr. Levin," Emily said. Adam shook his hand and stepped back to look at him.

The young man struck an attitude. A lock of his greasy dark hair fell into his eyes, eyes of a penetrating brightness, eyes that would look wonderful on screen, but only if Melpomene Moving Picture Studios was planning on filming the story of Rasputin, or Count Dracula, or Blackbeard the pirate. That face would not do for a simple cowboy.

Levin tilted his chin up and turned his profile toward the Weisses. That clinched it for Emily; he looked enough like Robert Montmorency to be his younger brother. Two faces like that in the same picture would be a disaster. The audience would become confused.

Maybe later.

"We'll call you," Emily said. Vera had to translate; alas, the finest actor in the northern hemisphere appeared to speak no English. He hunched his shoulders and skulked away toward the coffee bar. "But tell me, Vera, who is that?"

"Who is what?"

"The fair-haired young man in the corner. I thought he was with your party."

"He is friend of my Edward. Tomorrow he is going back to Finland, maybe organize some workers."

"I would very much like to have him in our movies," Emily said.

Adam blinked. "Why?"

"Oh, Adam, look at him. He's beautiful. The women will come flocking to see him in Melpomene's pictures."

"I bow to your expertise, my dear." She hated it when he called her "my dear" in that sarcastic tone, but there was no help for it. If Adam was unhappy because she knew a good-looking man when she saw one, it was just too bad. Had he or had he not given her complete authority over the casting decisions? Adam had no cause to be jealous of her admiration for this Finnish boy, for he surely knew himself to be even handsomer in her eyes. Years had passed since the days when Emily was a fool for yellow hair. Months anyway.

"I will have Edward introduce you to him," Vera said. At last the big one-eyed man finished gassing about his plans for a general strike. Vera brought Emily and Adam to him and introduced them with a proud smile. "Mr. and Mrs. Weiss, this is Edward Strawfield."

The name meant nothing to Emily, but Strawfield seemed to think he was important. Emily shook his hand and declared that she was delighted to meet him.

"Are you interested in the Movement?" he said.

"No, actually we're capitalists, Mr. Strawfield. Melpomene Pictures," Adam said.

"Miss Zinovia will be working in our movie company," Emily said.

47

"You're very lucky. Miss Zinovia is the best." He put his arm around the actress and squeezed her shoulders.

"Yes. Well," Adam said.

"Mr. Strawfield, I wonder whether you could introduce us to the young man in the corner. The one with the yellow hair," Emily said. "He would be perfect for one of the parts in our next picture."

"Erno Berg? He's not an actor."

"Just the same. I truly think we can use him."

They pushed their way through the press of Wobblies, anarchists, artists, and would-be free lovers to the small round table where Erno Berg sat contemplating his grimy knuckles by the light of the dripping candle. "He's leaving for Finland tomorrow," Strawfield said. "I don't think he'll be interested. Here! Erno! These two nice people want to talk to you."

The young man stood up, revealing himself to be tall and well-formed, with broad shoulders and slim hips. He looked at Emily with eyes the color of the sea after a storm has passed — those cheekbones! that mouth! — and said something to Strawfield in Finnish. Strawfield replied in the same language.

"I don't know," the young man said. "I

want to go to Finland tomorrow."

"Stay for a few weeks longer," Emily said. "Try it. You can always use more money when you get to Finland. We'll pay you well."

"I don't act."

"You'll be fine," Emily said. "It isn't as though we're asking you to go on the stage. It's only a few little movies."

"A few little movies," he repeated. "And the pay is how much?"

Adam named a figure.

"All right, then."

"We begin shooting tomorrow morning," Adam said. "In Fort Lee. Meet us at the 128th Street ferry slip at eight. All the other actors will be there."

FIVE

The 128th Street ferry slip smelled like low tide, dead fish, unwashed people, excrement, and garbage, but to Emily Weiss it was all as bracing as some rare perfume. Barely retaining her huge fashionable hat in the wind that came howling off the Hudson, she snuggled up to Adam in his Norfolk jacket and plus fours (he had assured her that the costume was the only correct thing for a moving picture director to wear) and scanned the crowd for her actors.

The first to appear was Robert Montmorency, his smart homburg and lowering dark brows coming into view just over the heads of the ordinary people crowding the ferry slip. How furtive he looked. Surely his posture was better than that onstage. He turned up his coat collar against the sting of the wind and gazed all around, searching for her, she supposed. She waved; when he saw her he threw back his shoulders, sucked in his stomach, and pulled himself up very straight. The whites of his eyes were blood-shot. Why, Emily thought, I believe the man is hungover. So the rumors about his drinking are true.

Emily shivered. She still missed her fur coat. The smile Montmorency gave her was almost warm enough to make up for it, if a trifle forced. When he took her gloved hand and kissed the back of it she could feel her cheeks redden. Continental manners still flustered her. Fighting to appear noncha-lant, she introduced him to Adam, who shook his hand and muttered, "Mont-morency," rather coldly.

Montmorency cleared his throat. "Please understand that for the purposes of moving pictures I call myself Robert Chalmers."

"We'll call you Chalmers, then," Adam said. "That's easily done. But I thought you'd never been in pictures before."

"As Robert Montmorency, never. Under other names, yes. But after all, 'What's in a name? That which we call a rose by any other word would smell as sweet.' " His smile would have been more engaging without the liquor on his breath, or if his teeth were in better shape.

"What pictures did you appear in?" Adam asked him.

"I can't recall."

"I guess they must have smelled pretty sweet," Adam said.

The actor lifted his shoulders, something between a shrug and a shudder. Emily, too, wondered about the false name. Clearly he was ashamed to appear in moving pictures. A legitimate theater snob. "Never mind, Adam," Emily said. "Mr. Mon . . . er . . . Chalmers is an extremely competent actor. We're lucky to have him. Anyone can find himself in a flop. Remember *Monkey Days?*"

The actor's face lit up. Perhaps he was thinking of the lovely Myrtle, who danced in the chorus beside Emily; Myrtle, who had been madly in love with him for a week and a half, although behind his back she called him "Fast-handed Bob." But, no, he was remembering Emily herself. "Mrs. Weiss! You were in *Monkey Days!* Emily Daggett, wasn't it? Back row, third girl from the left. I remember you well."

"You have a sharp eye, Mr. Mon — Mr. Chalmers."

"I had an engagement in Philadelphia myself at the time, but I saw your show. Miss Myrtle Stirrup was a dear friend of mine. An enchanting creature, Myrtle." He sighed. "She threw me over for a silver baron."

"Tough break," Adam said.

"It was all for the best."

Adam handed him his copy of the scenario. "You'll want to look this over before we start." Montmorency — Chalmers — riffled through the script.

"You'll be playing Black Bart," Emily said.

"There's really nothing to it," Adam said. "Just fool with your mustache."

Chalmers turned away and hunched over the script, seemingly lost in the plot of *Revenge in the Saddle.* His right hand began to twitch, and then it crept toward his pants pocket, where Emily was almost certain she saw a bulge the size and shape of a pint flask. He turned toward them again and said, with a cheery smile, "May I have my ticket? I'd like to go on board the ferry and study this."

Go on board the ferry and drink, you mean. Emily shook her head. "Wait for our cameraman. If he's not there to take the pictures, we can't afford to take a company of actors to Fort Lee. It would be a pointless waste of money."

"But surely we can use the time to rehearse," Chalmers said.

Adam and Emily had discussed rehearsals, but Adam had insisted that rehearsals were an unnecessary luxury, given the short time they had to finish the pictures. They were silent movies, after all. The director could simply stand behind the camera and shout at the actors until the desired effect was achieved. Everyone worked that way.

"No time to rehearse," Adam said.

Chalmers searched first one, then the other of their faces, his own face a mask of dismay. "Not rehearse?"

"Don't look so pale, Mr. Mon — Chalmers," Emily said. "At least there will be no lines to learn."

"But —"

Happily the other actors arrived, providing a distraction. First to appear was Erno Berg. "Mr. Berg! Over here," Emily called. As he approached she realized she had never seen her young pet walking. In motion he was stiff, even awkward. Perhaps with rehearsal he might . . . but, no, there was to be no rehearsal.

Vera Zinovia stood at the pier entrance embracing Big Ed Strawfield. The two held each other as if for the last time. When he released her the girl turned and came toward the ferry, biting her handkerchief. Her mascara was running.

"Vera!" Emily called. "Here we are, over here. What's wrong? Is Mr. Strawfield going away?"

"We never know. Edward says forces of capitalism could swoop down upon him momentarily. Anything is possible." She dabbed at her eyes with the blackened scrap of lace. Chalmers winced at her heavily accented English. Emily wanted to kick him. Who cared what the actors sounded like? This was film. Nobody would hear them.

Adam took the girl's little hand and shook it. He did not put it to his lips, although he gave Emily a sidelong glance as if to say "How would you like it?"

"Tell me about your acting experience, Miss Zinovia," Adam said. She reeled off a number of plays she had starred in with the Moscow Art Theater, Chekhov and Ibsen mostly, but also a part in *The Brothers Karamazov.*

"The Moscow Art Theater. I suppose you worked with that rank charlatan, Stanislavsky," Chalmers said to her.

"I beg your pardon. Konstantin Sergeyevich is foremost genius of modern theater."

"Modern theater. Modern claptrap," Chalmers said. Miss Zinovia's little gloved hands became claws. Before she could spring at Chalmers's face Emily thrust a copy of the scenario at her.

"This is the script for *Revenge in the*

Saddle," she said. "Tell them about the plot, Adam."

"I see this picture as a modern morality tale," Adam said.

Chalmers's eyes glazed over. "Do tell."

"I think you'll find the artistic quality very high. Our scenario is loosely based on the story of *The Virginian.*"

"A dime novel," Chalmers said.

"Hardly that, sir, I'm sure I paid at least a dollar for my copy. At any rate, you will be playing Black Bart, the evil rancher. Erno Berg, the noble cowboy, is your enemy; he is infatuated with Miss Zinovia, who plays your daughter, but in truth his heart belongs to the wholesome schoolmarm, Fay Winningly."

"Deathless."

"Yes, well, that's the main conflict. You fight with him over cards. Miss Zinovia, your character pretends to try to patch up the quarrel, while in reality . . ."

Emily's Indians joined them then, dressed in denim with their long hair tied at the nape of the neck. How beautifully they moved. Perhaps they could give Erno lessons. Then Adam's cameraman arrived with his apparatus on his shoulder, the signal for them all to board the ferry. And not a moment too soon. The deckhands were casting off the hawsers when little Fay Winningly appeared on the dock, radiant in her honey-colored sausage curls.

"Oh, please wait!" she cried, but wait they would not. Chalmers rushed down the ramp and rescued her. "Fast-handed Bob," indeed. He reached across the gap between the ferry and the shore and scooped her into his arms, with her golden hair flying all around her shoulders.

"Thank you, kind sir," she twinkled at him. He seemed reluctant to put her down.

Then as her feet touched the deck the cameraman uttered a groan and jumped behind a post, hiding himself from the shore. Staring across the churning green-brown water at them stood a stocky, balding man in a checkered suit, his face contorted with malevolence.

"Duffy," the cameraman muttered. "How the hell did he find us?"

"Who is this Duffy?" Emily said.

"Seamus Duffy. Edison's man. One of the Trust detectives. Well, I suppose it could be worse."

"How could it be worse?" Adam said.

"The old plaster could have sent McCoy."

The cast and crew of Melpomene Moving Picture Studios gained the opposite shore

57

of the Hudson without further hindrance from the minions of Thomas Edison. Nevertheless, all during the trolley ride up the cliff from the ferry landing to the little town of Fort Lee, Emily Weiss felt stirrings of irrational terror. To be rising higher and higher up the side of the Palisades, to see the river so far below and the ferrymen scurrying like ants, made her feel that the trolley might tip over at any moment and go hurtling off the cliff. The feeling was insane; she could not explain it, although she knew she had felt it before. Could it be that she had died of a long fall in another life? She moved across the aisle and took a seat next to the solid, friendly hillside.

Instead of looking out across the blue void toward the city Emily looked at the dark striated rock that made up the face of the cliff, the small trees growing out of the cracks between the layers, the branches of the trees, most of them bare, but some with withered brown leaves that rustled as they passed. The hill seemed very solid.

"What's wrong?" Adam said.

"Nothing, darling," she lied. It occurred to her that her terror of heights had increased, rather than abated, since her marriage to Adam. It occurred to her further that running the Melpomene Moving Picture Studios was a huge responsibility. The fate of all these people was in her hands, hers and Adam's, and their fate was in the hands of these people. The Indians, completely inexperienced as actors. Vera Zinovia, so high-strung that she could not bear to be separated from her lover, even for a few hours. "Fast-handed Bob," who would have to be closely watched for drinking and groping. And Erno Berg. What a face! What a body! What little they knew about him! When Emily tried to find out what he had done before she found him in the Café Boheme, he lapsed into a stream of Finnish. She assumed he was a laborer of some sort, but she didn't know for sure. She thought he was about nineteen years of age, but she didn't know that, either.

And the lovely Fay, with her waiflike air of innocence and her lily of the valley cologne, sitting next to Adam now. He must have said something funny, for the two of them were laughing to kill themselves. Fay looked up and saw Emily watching them, moved her hand quickly back into her own lap and composed her features. How Emily itched to slap her. Perhaps she would get a chance later on.

The trolley let them off in the middle of the town of Fort Lee, so quiet you would never know how close you were to the metropolis across the Hudson: the main street paved in dirt, the clapboard houses in their weedy yards needing paint, a few shops with striped awnings, a pungent livery stable, and a small white-painted hotel. On the hotel veranda, rocking chairs nodded and bobbed in the November wind. Emily liked the chairs. It would be pleasant to sit in one of them on a fine day with a pad and pencil on her knee and the sun in her face and write scenarios.

Today, however, what they needed from the hotel was two dressing rooms, one for the men and one for the women. She went inside to take care of it while Adam and Mr. Johnson discussed where to begin shooting.

The hotel lobby smelled faintly of mold and wood smoke. A good fire was burning in the fieldstone fireplace. On a small table before the fireplace a thing sat that was like a wooden coffee grinder with a hearing trumpet attached to it: an Edison cylinder phonograph. Softly a tune whined from the apparatus, rather like a chorus of gnats. Emily recognized the "Dill Pickle Rag." On the mantel a Carpenter gothic clock ticktocked, but not in time to the music. Over the back of an overstuffed brown plush chair the pink top of a man's head shone through a white fringe of hair. Drifting smoke came not from the fireplace but from the man's pipe. The effect was profoundly peaceful.

Emily let the storm door close behind her; it made a little bang. Startled, the man stood up and turned to face her. His face was like a friendly pink pudding.

"Good morning, young lady," he said. "Something I can do for you?"

"I'm Emily Weiss. I'm here in town with a movie company, Melpomene Moving Pictures, and we would like to rent two rooms today for our actors to dress and make up in, if that's possible."

"I'm Martin Potts. My wife and I own this hotel. I think we might find you a couple of rooms. Not many New York City tourists this time of year."

What rosy cheeks. That face would work well on film. "Maybe you'd like to be in one of our pictures," she said. "We'll be needing some extras."

"Movies," Mr. Potts said. "How about that." He checked her in at the desk and showed her the two rooms. She put her actors in them with instructions to make up and costume themselves for a Western.

The hotel may have kept a roaring fire going in the main hall, but the actors complained that the rooms upstairs were miserable, damp, and freezing. Dressing and making up proceeded at a crawl. The cold cream and greasepaint had to be melted over a candle before they could be spread on the actors' faces, and on their backs as well, in the case of Fred and Billy Parker, who, being Indians, were to appear in the first scene without shirts. The boys had brought their own red greasepaint with them, fortunately.

"We know all about show business," Fred said. "Our uncle is with the Miller Brother's Hundred 'n' One Wild West Show."

"Greasepaint is good," Billy said. "Keeps you almost as warm as a shirt."

The so-called Indian color would not make a great deal of difference on camera, although the shade, an artificial sort of brick red, was nothing like Billy's own deeply tanned skin. "You'll see when you develop the film," Mr. Johnson said to Emily. "There are colors that the film won't pick up. They look black. What you want is to have a lot of contrast between light and dark."

Only Erno Berg came unprepared with greasepaint. He would have to be made up, or else no moving picture camera could capture his facial expressions, with his pale skin and his brows and lashes like corn silk. Fay volunteered to paint him. "I know what the camera needs," she said. Emily left the Finnish boy in the actress's hands and went downstairs to get warm.

"Awfully cold out there," Mr. Johnson said. He began to load his camera in front of the fire.

"You don't think it's too cold to shoot, do you?" Emily said.

"Not for me. I've got an alcohol lamp built into the camera to warm the film so it keeps winding smoothly. You might want to build a fire where we're shooting to warm up the actors, though. Well, Mr. Weiss. What do we shoot first?"

"The card-playing scene," Adam said. "We'll shoot it on the front porch of the hotel."

Mr. Johnson went out to the porch, calculated where the edges of the frame would fall and marked them off with rope to guide the actors. Emily fastened the big M for Melpomene to the porch railing. The actors came out and took their places for the scene, looking almost clownish in their makeup. Adam put his megaphone to his lips.

"Action!"

And so the little company played the scene while Mr. Johnson cranked the camera, the very first scene of the very first moving picture of the Melpomene Moving Picture Studios. There never was a more wooden cowboy than Erno Berg, but Mr. Chalmers did enough acting for both of them. He postured, he sneered, he curled his lip and his black mustache as well, and in a climax of scenery-chewing passion he threw his cards in Erno Berg's stony painted face. Fred and Billy lounged against the stucco wall of the hotel without shirts, dressing the set as wild Indians, shivering slightly in the November wind. Fay and Vera, their eyes ringed with kohl, held each other's hands and mimed intense interest in the card game, as did Adam's extras — Mr. Potts, his plump, jolly wife, his thin, gloomy hired girl, and his wiry old stable hand. There was enough tension in the scene to carry the entire one-reeler, especially at the end, when the ferry whistle blew and Adam began to shout, "Speed it up! Speed it up! Seamus Duffy is coming to break the camera and close us down! Stand up now, Erno!"

Erno stood up. It was all he was required to do in the scene, and he did it very effectively. The muscles in his shoulders rippled. His shadow fell across Mr. Chalmers, who was half a head shorter. And so the scene ended.

"Aaand cut!" Adam said. "Well done,

people! Now let's get out of here before the detective arrives. We'll do the scenes in the woods now. Come on! Emily, clean up those cards, will you? And the front of the hotel. Meet us later." He grabbed the Melpomene trademark and off they all went flying northward at a dead run, Adam, Mr. Johnson and his camera, Robert Chalmers, Erno Berg, the Indians, Vera Zinovia with her gypsy shawl streaming in the wind, and little Fay Winningly tripping in her fashionable shoes, her curls bouncing behind her.

Emily picked up the cards. Then she saw what Adam meant about cleaning the front of the hotel. Billy, in leaning against the wall, had left a perfect red print of himself in greasepaint. It might as well have been a sign reading WESTERN MOVIES SHOT HERE.

She was still scrubbing it off when two men got off the trolley. Neither one of them was the dreaded Seamus Duffy, although they both looked like detectives. The tall one moved with dignified deliberation, the shorter man with tense, contained energy. If they were dogs they would have been a Great Dane and a bull terrier. Both of them cast their eyes all around, taking in everything. More trouble from Edison and the Trust. I will dissemble, Emily thought, and assumed an expression of slack-jawed stupidity. Fortunately she had left her expensive hat inside.

"Hey, girlie," the bull terrier said.

"Pardon me?"

"I'm looking for a guy. I wonder if you've seen him."

"No way of telling."

"He's about five eleven, bald head, might have been wearing a plaid suit and a derby hat."

"I haven't seen him, no."

"You must have seen the movie company, though," said the Great Dane. His voice was deep and resonant, much more attractive than the bull terrier's New York City guttural grunting.

"Nope."

The bull terrier said, "Don't give us that stuff, sister. You came over on the ferry with a movie company. I saw you. Where are they working?" (He actually said "woiking.")

"I came over on the ferry to clean the hotel, which is my job. I don't know about any movie people."

"You couldn't miss 'em. There was a guy with a camera and a tripod over his shoulder."

"Oh, them," she said. "When they got off the ferry they went that way." She pointed southward.

"Thank you very much, miss," the Great Dane said. A beautiful voice, and he carried himself well, too. That man is wasted as a detective, Emily thought, he should be on the stage. The men left without appearing to notice the actor-shaped stain she was working on.

Six

Nothing could have been more ideal for developing film than the windowless bathroom of Adam and Emily's digs in the Knickerbocker. The sink was plenty big, as was the dressing table, and the hanging light fixture was within easy reach, enabling Adam to replace the regular lightbulb with a red one. In its scarlet glow Emily watched her husband mixing chemicals, timing processes, and washing film until she felt that she could develop the film herself.

The only drawback to living in their laboratory was the smell of chemicals. Adam and Emily became accustomed to it, but the chambermaid accosted Adam in the hall and complained about it loudly and insistently, until he perceived that he must buy her silence. He slipped her a twenty and tipped her a wink, and that was that. Still they were forced to eat downstairs in the restaurant rather than risk the discovery of their activities by the room service waiter. There was only so much money in the budget for bribes.

The walls of the room did not make a good projection screen, covered as they were with flowers and little Chinese people, but a sheet from their bed, pulled tight over the bathroom door, served the purpose very well. When the positive print was dry Adam lay on the bed in his underwear smoking a Lucky Strike, blowing occasional smoke rings, while Emily ran the day's output through the projector.

A feeling was stealing over her that she was born for this, to make moving pictures. She had never felt more alive. Beautiful faces flickering in the dark. Smoke from Adam's cigarette drifting across the shadow images. They had shot nearly five hundred feet of film, enough thrilling footage for half of a one-reel Western.

"We'll shoot the rest of the picture tomorrow, if the weather holds. You were right about the Indians, Emily. They photograph superbly."

"Not only do they look good on film, darling, but they're useful offscreen. I'm giving them an extra three dollars a day to keep our Mr. Chalmers sober."

"How do they keep him sober?"

"They pester him for acting lessons so that he hasn't time to drink. He's teaching Fred to fence."

"So far so good," Adam said. "I noticed he was still on his feet by the end of the day."

"By the way, there were two more detectives nosing around after you left the hotel this morning. I think they were working with Duffy. I pretended I was a cleaning woman and sent them in the wrong direction."

"Good girl. Say, back the film up, will you? To the place where Vera makes her entrance." Emily cranked the handle around the other way. Vera walked backward and hovered at the edge of the frame, bathing the camera in her smoldering gaze. "She looks good, don't you think? I love the way she moves."

Emily had to agree. "How do you suppose she can chew her pearls like that without getting lipstick all over them?"

"It must be a Russian thing," Adam said. "This guy Stanislavsky taught her a lot. I'm surprised that little Fay can run in those shoes." Fay's tiny delicate pumps were the height of fashion, perhaps too womanly for her girlish role. Emily was hoping that no one would notice her feet. In the costumes she designed Emily was working for broad effects. Fay's flowing hair and the obvious lack of a corset under her pinafore would carry the message.

"Roll it again, sweetheart. Vera's entrance." Emily turned the crank. Vera undulated across the corral — actually a farmyard a little way outside of Fort Lee — like some irresistible force of nature, say a tidal wave, to work her wiles on the shy hero. Erno stood waiting for her like a rock. Well, that was his style, rocklike. But he was so handsome.

"We should get her under contract," Emily said, "before some other company hires her away. She's very good. Him, too. Don't you think he looks fine on camera?"

"Fine," Adam said, and blew out a stream of smoke.

Suddenly Vera's skirts became entangled in the Melpomene trademark. It flopped around and looked cheap, like the cheesy piece of cardboard it was. Vera tugged herself loose and went on with the scene. Emily had meant to replace the cardboard M with a wooden one, but she couldn't find anybody who could whittle. Right now it was fastened to a hardwood stake, the better to pull it up in a hurry and run away if

71

Edison's detectives discovered them working.

Adam groaned. "Who put the trademark right there?"

"Erno, I guess," Emily said. "The ground is frozen, you know. I'm not strong enough myself to do it. I gave it to Mr. Chalmers, but he curled his lip at me and asked if he looked like a prop boy. We should probably have a prop boy, Adam. Do you want to reshoot the scene?"

"No, just snip that bit out and glue the film together. I really want to finish this one tomorrow, if it's sunny, and start on the next movie. And see that you mount the trademark on something a little more substantial. Maybe a sharpened iron rod."

"Right, chief. But, you know, we're going to have to do something more substantial about Duffy and his friends. I can't simply keep misdirecting them. Sooner or later they'll stop paying attention to anything I tell them."

"You want me to beat them up?" He gave her a long, cool stare. In his sleeveless undershirt he was wiry — and wildly attractive — but perhaps not bulky enough to overcome a professional tough.

"No, dear, not you, but I was talking to Vera."

"Vera. Good idea. She can ensnare Duffy and his friends in her toils, one by one, and force them to kill themselves."

"Good scenario. No, what I meant was that Vera is involved with Big Ed Strawfield. You remember Big Ed."

"The king of the Wobblies," Adam said.

"The same. Vera says a few of Big Ed's Wobbly friends are out of work right now. I told her we would hire them as security."

"I hope you aren't telling me you hired a crew of labor thugs to protect us against Thomas Edison."

"It'll be all right, Adam. They all have their own plaid flannel shirts. We can use them as extras in the mob scene."

"A mob of Wobblies."

"Perhaps you would like to fire them and hire some more acceptable extras for the mob scene. You can explain to them why you find them so objectionable."

"No, no, my dear. I have no objection to Reds, per se, as long as they behave themselves. I trust you didn't tell them to murder Mr. Edison's detectives."

"Of course not. That is to say, I haven't talked to them yet. They're supposed to meet us at the ferry slip tomorrow, if it's sunny, and then I'll give them their instructions."

"Which will be what?"

"I'll tell them to distract any detectives who come following us, that's all. Distract them. Lead them astray. Or beat them up. But only as a last resort. Then they can all put on their flannel shirts and meet us in Fort Lee in time for the mob scene in the second picture. I promise it will work beautifully."

At eight the next morning the company gathered once again at the ferry slip under a cloudless sky.

Seven men stood shoulder to shoulder with Vera Zinovia's beau, Big Ed Strawfield, at the entrance to the ferry slip. Strawfield, in his flat black trilby hat, with his hands like hams and his milky colored bad right eye; the Wobblies in their cloth caps, chins up, fists clenched, muscles bulging — all of them might have been posing for a Red propaganda poster.

Emily handed Vera Zinovia her ferry ticket and said, "Thank you so much for getting your friends to help us. It's important for us to finish the pictures on time. I don't know what we would do if we had no defense against Mr. Edison and his detectives."

"Edward is very good to me," Vera said. "If I am in picture, he will do anything to

74

make picture a success."

An unlikely couple, Emily would have said. "Where did you two meet each other?"

"In Moscow. Edward was there on a speaking tour to promote the Movement. He came to theater one night."

"He saw you in a play."

"Ibsen. Edward did not like Ibsen, but he liked me. He sent me flowers. We met for supper. A very sweet man. We have been violently in love ever since."

"How long has that been?"

"Three years."

"And yet you don't marry. Forgive me, it's not my business."

"I am not offended. Marriage is bourgeois institution," Vera said. "A piece of paper. A list of obligations imposed by the state, not relevant. Edward and I belong to each other. This is all the world needs to know."

It sounded like something Emma Goldman would say. "You may be right at that." Emily looked at the brutish Ed Strawfield with new eyes. A lover. How charming. The very sweet man was giving last-minute instructions to his Wobblies, scowling, slamming his right fist into his left palm.

It was time for Emily to explain to this man that the outright murder of any detectives would be way beyond what the situation required. Some pieces of paper from the state were more important than others, for example arrest warrants. She trotted out to the entrance to the ferry slip and introduced herself.

"Mrs. Weiss!" he said. "Nice to see you."

"May I have a word with you, Mr. Strawfield?"

"Certainly." A private word was out of the question in the midst of this crowd, but he stepped to the edge of the dock with her, out of the stream of traffic and away from his men. Green water, lumpy with orange rinds and filth, sloshed against the greasy pilings. Emily pulled her muffler up to her cheekbones against the wind.

"Vera is good, isn't she?" Strawfield said. "There's nobody like her in the movies."

"Yes, she's lovely. A fine actress. Mr. Strawfield, I want to make sure you understand about these detectives," she said.

"Understand what?"

"Don't hurt them. I mean, particularly, don't kill them. Okay?"

"Mrs. Weiss, you shouldn't believe everything you read in the papers," he said.

"What would I read in the papers?"

He frowned, as if he thought she was playing a joke on him. "You don't know?"

"I can't say I do."

"I suppose you never heard of the trial of the century. It was only two years ago."

As everyone knew, the trial of the century was all about the murder of Stanford White, the famous architect, by the husband of Evelyn Nesbit, the famous beauty White had gone to bed with. Emily stared at this threadbare gorilla who called himself Ed Strawfield. "You're not Harry Thaw. He's a tiny little rich man."

"No. The other trial of the century."

"I guess I missed it."

"You're joking, of course. In any case I was innocent, Mrs. Weiss; I was not the mastermind of the murder of Governor Steunenberg; they couldn't pin that on me, not that I didn't believe he deserved to die, or the boxcar full of scabs either, may they rot."

"So you're not a murderer," she said, wondering whether to believe it. *Boxcar full of scabs?*

"Twelve good men and true accepted the word of Mr. Clarence Darrow. And my word, I might add," he said.

"I'm sure I could do no less. But, listen, Mr. Strawfield, whatever you may or may not have done in the past, don't murder any of these detectives. It would be bad for Melpomene Moving Picture Studios. It would be bad for Vera and her career. Just keep them from crossing the river after us."

He gave as good an impression of wide-eyed innocence as a man can with only one functioning eye. "We won't harm a hair of their heads, Mrs. Weiss. We'll simply fix it so they never reach Fort Lee. You go ahead, get on the ferry with the movie company. Leave the rest to the IWW."

"Try not to break the law, Mr. Strawfield." Big Ed gave a hollow laugh. His merriment was more frightening than his scowl. Emily stepped aboard the ferry, and then turned to look back.

Here came Mr. Johnson in hot haste. Strawfield's Wobblies parted to let him through, then closed again as Duffy came across the street behind him.

Johnson jumped aboard the ferry. The whistle hooted. Duffy stood looking from one face to the other of the men who were blocking his way. Emily could see him trying to pass them; she could see him reasoning with them; she could see him pulling out a roll of bills, peeling a few off, and offering them to the Wobblies while Big Ed Strawfield stood with his hands on his hips and laughed at him.

The ferry churned away from the dock. The Wobblies closed around Duffy. Now he was screaming, his voice clearly audible out on the river, even over the sound of the ferry's engine. Then a plume of water rose into the air, followed by the sound of a splash. So much for Duffy. Emily hoped he wasn't killed. Even if he wasn't killed, even if he didn't catch pneumonia and have to go to bed for two weeks — please let him catch pneumonia, then Melpomene Studios could finish all four pictures — even if he didn't, it would be hours before he found dry clothes and got after them again.

SEVEN

They shot the last scene of *Revenge in the Saddle* at eleven thirty that morning. The scenario called for Erno, on horseback, to hoist little Fay onto the saddle in front of him and ride the elderly gelding they had rented from Potts's livery stable into the setting sun, which would have been in the west, beyond the woods, if the sun had actually been setting. Erno mounted the horse awkwardly, climbing onto its back from a peeled-log fence rail. Erno reached for Fay's waist, but, alas, he knew so little about riding that even that ancient and dispirited horse shied and tried to bite him.

Adam frowned at Emily. "Did this guy tell you he could ride when you hired him?"

"I thought for sure he could ride." Sitting in the coffeehouse, he looked very much like a cowboy to Emily. "Don't you think he looks like a cowboy?"

"Johnson! *Cut!* . . . You thought for sure he

could act, too, didn't you, sweetheart?"

"He looks good. Why should he act? Maybe the horse hates Fay." Emily could understand that.

"I think, my dear, that neither one of your Western stars has ever seen a horse. Erno! Get down off that horse. We'll have you and Fay walk away hand in hand, and you can lead it by the reins. You *can* lead a horse, can't you?"

Erno's face turned red under the makeup. "The horse is upset," he said. "It's the noise."

"What noise?" Adam said.

"Hammering. Sawing. Loud noises make horses nervous."

Big Ed Strawfield and his Wobblies, happy to get the extra pay Adam offered them to serve as carpenters (union scale), were throwing together the façade of a jailhouse that was to be torn down in the mob scene of the second movie. The clamor was so deafening that Adam and Emily no longer heard it. How could it bother a horse? "Next the actors will be wanting a string quartet," Adam said.

"Biograph uses a string quartet," Fay said.

"Biograph can afford to pay a string quartet. Roll the camera, Johnson! Aaand . . . action!" Slowly Erno and Fay strolled down the road, hand in hand, into the leafless trees. The horse followed along, all sweet obedience. When its rump disappeared behind the hill, Adam bellowed, "Aaand . . . cut!"

"That's it, then," Emily said.

Adam beamed. "That's it for *Revenge in the Saddle.* Three more pictures to go. Get the film from Johnson, and hide it, in case the detectives show up. We'll give the players half an hour to eat and change costumes and then we'll set up for the mob scene in *Lynching at Laramie.*"

"Right, chief," Emily said.

"I'll buy everybody lunch. I feel like celebrating."

A smiling Mrs. Potts prepared the dining room for them. Mrs. Potts was the female equivalent of her plump white-haired husband, except that she bustled about enveloped in the smell of bread dough rather than pipe tobacco. She pushed four square tables together end to end and spread them with a long checkered cloth. The movie company pulled up chairs and arranged themselves along the table while Mrs. Potts and the thin little hired girl brought them roast ham, mashed potatoes, bread and butter, boiled greens, and at last a selection of fruit pies.

Emily sat at the foot of the table, Adam at the head, mother and father. Fay, the bad baby, sat between Erno and Mr. Chalmers, twinkling at them alternately, doing heaven knew what with them under the table. Big Ed Strawfield sat next to Erno; the two conversed in sober streams of Finnish. How many languages was a serious labor leader expected to speak nowadays? Truly Big Ed was a man of unexpected accomplishments. Vera, on Big Ed's right, nibbled a piece of bread and looked tragic. The Indians addressed themselves in silence to their food.

Across from the actors sat the seven Wobblies. Emily had trouble telling them apart. She tried to engage the one next to her in conversation, in the belief that he would have philosophical things to say about the labor movement, but he merely grunted and continued to gobble his food down. She turned her attention to Mr. Johnson, sitting between her and Vera.

"So, Mr. Johnson, I understand you used to work for Mr. Thomas Edison."

"Yep."

"What's he like?"

"He's a genius." Johnson took a bite of ham and chewed it for a long time. Emily thought that would be all the conversation she got out of him, but at last he swallowed and said, "And an old plaster."

"How so?"

"Mrs. Weiss, the movies could be better than they are."

"I suppose you're right."

"What I mean is, sure, there's a lot of money in movies, but that's not the most interesting thing about movies. It's what they could be. Less like a sideshow. More like books."

"Books?"

"Yes, ma'am. Now, you take books. Suppose Thomas Alva Edison got to tell people what they were allowed to write about, then put his name on the cover of every book and took a cut of the profits, all because he claimed to have invented paper."

One of the Wobblies spoke up. "He never invented paper. I seen some books older than he is."

"If Mr. Edison's patent lawyers got hold of the idea he invented paper, you'd see his name on the cover of the Holy Bible," Johnson said.

"So is it that he wants the money, or that he wants artistic control?" Emily said.

"Artistic control of the Bible?" the Wobbly said. "That don't seem right."

"It's a figure of speech," Johnson said.

"I'm trying to say the old plaster is a drag on progress. The movies coming out of the Edison studios aren't as good as Europe an movies, or even the movies from Biograph, the company that beat his lawyers in court and then joined the Trust."

"You're saying he's no artist."

"He's a great inventor. He's no artist."

"What was it like to work for him?" Emily wondered.

"Exciting. Dangerous. I hate to tell you how many men in the shop were poisoned by mercury. Say, Mrs. Weiss, are you going to finish that?"

"No. Help yourself. I seldom eat more than one slice of ham."

"I was lucky to get out of there alive, fact is. The old, er, Mr. Edison was never bothered by the mercury, or the weather, or anything else. He has the constitution of an ox. People dropped dead to the right and left of him, and still he carried on. But we were all thrilled whenever one of his ideas came out right." Johnson fell silent and addressed his mashed potatoes.

"The Edison Machine Works was a union shop, wasn't it?" the Wobbly said. "What was the union doing while all these men were being poisoned?"

"The lab assistants weren't union. Only

the skilled workers. And when they got too big for their britches Mr. Edison fooled them into going out on strike, and then moved the whole works to Schenectady without them."

At the word *strike* all the Wobblies turned to listen, some of them pausing with their forks halfway to their lips.

"How can you fool people into going on strike?" Emily said.

"You do it by being as tricky as a fox." Johnson now had the attention of everyone at the table.

"Ninety members of the electrical workers union manufactured lightbulbs in Edison's shop on Goerck Street. Very skilled work. One of them got Mr. Edison to hire his son for an office boy.

"The boy didn't step lively enough to please Mr. Edison, so he fired him. But the electrical workers weren't having any of that. They said they'd walk out if he didn't take the boy back. At the time the sale of lightbulbs was making Mr. Edison most of his money. He still needed these men. So he didn't make a fuss; he just smiled and gave the boy his job back. After that the kid just got ruder and lazier. But every night Mr. Edison went up to the third floor of his factory and worked on a lightbulb-making machine that could be operated by an unskilled worker. Every night. You know, he never sleeps."

"I've heard rumors to that effect," Emily said.

"When he thought he had the machine the way he wanted it he tried it out on a couple of unskilled workers, I think they were bums that he found drinking under a bridge. Sneaked them up to the third floor and got them making lightbulbs. They said it was the easiest work they ever did. Then he took out a patent on the lightbulb-making machine."

"Well, naturally," Emily said.

"Naturally. Edison never fails to secure the patents, least of all on the things he actually invents himself. Then he had his most trusted men run up thirty or forty more lightbulb making machines. As soon as they got the new machines working, Mr. Edison went down to his office and fired the boy."

"Poor little fellow," Emily said. "How surprised he must have been."

"It was the beginning of his education, for certain," Mr. Johnson said. "When the skilled workers got the news they walked off the job to a man." The Wobblies all grunted. Mr. Johnson gulped down the dregs of his coffee. "They never went back; Mr. Edison didn't need them anymore. Moved the whole operation to Schenectady. He's patient, he's ruthless, and he never sleeps."

Mrs. Potts brought another pot of coffee to the table, dispelling the specter of Thomas Edison, and the moviemakers cheerfully passed it around. Emily contemplated the table with satisfaction, the big happy movie family of Melpomene. An empire of her very own. Only the sleepless Thomas Edison posed any threat to them, Edison and the weather, which might turn too dark to film, or the actors, who might fall into jealous fits over Fay, or Howie Kazanow, who might foreclose on the whole shebang before they could make a long-term success of it. But for now, it was a short-term success, with ample cause for rejoicing: the first movie finished, their bellies full, and nobody openly hating anybody else.

"All right, people, half an hour to get ready for the mob scene of *Lynching at Laramie*," Adam said. "You have your copies of the scenario. We'll meet in the stable yard at twelve thirty." With a great scraping of chairs they all left to make their preparations. Adam came around the table and kissed Emily on top of the head.

"Come with me, sweetheart."

"What?"

"I found a piece of land for sale. It would be ideal for a studio." He took her hand and pulled her toward the door.

She grabbed her coat and hat on the way past the cloakroom. "A studio!"

"Arc lights, indoor scenery, dressing rooms, a place to store your costumes —"

"All very well, but where are we going to get the money?"

"When we give Howie Kazanow his four pictures, we'll have the money."

"Of course."

"The lot is up this hill, about a half mile up the road. There's a shortcut through these woods, with a nice view of the river." The path rose sharply. Adam climbed straight up, and Emily followed him. Presently a gust of wind threatened to take her hat.

"Wait," she said. "I must readjust my hat pin."

"How many birds gave their lives for that hat, Emily? You should wear ribbons, the way Fay does."

"Ribbons won't keep my little head warm," she said, mumbling through hairpins.

"But your hair! Surely that will keep your

little head warm."

The hair all secured, she replaced the hat. "I wear this hat because a girl never knows when she'll need a stout hat pin." She anchored the pin firmly through the knot of hair on top of her head. They continued climbing.

"You're under my protection now, Emily. You're my wife. You'll never need hat pins again."

"Yes, I'll need hat pins to keep my hat on in the wind, my darling."

"Not if you wear a different sort of hat. Look at Vera. Her hat fits closely over her head."

"Her hat looks like a feed bag with a silk flower on it."

"And yours looks like a dishpan covered with dead birds."

"I never knew you didn't like my hats."

"The point is, sweetheart, that no wife of mine will ever have to use a hat pin as a weapon."

They continued climbing. Emily realized that anger made her heart beat faster. "Have you heard about the English judge who ordered the suffragettes not to wear hats with hat pins, so as to keep them from being able to defend themselves?" Adam stopped and turned to look at her.

In the movies, when a director wanted to show an emotion clearly, he had the actor hold a stare for what in real life would be a long time. This was real life, Emily would have thought, but Adam gave her a movie stare. "My God! You're a suffragette?"

"Maybe I am. Why shouldn't I be? I certainly won't be subjugated."

A grimace passed across his face, the same look the noble hero wore in the latest nickelodeon hit, *Her Wretched Indiscretion.* How true were the movies? How true should they be? Was there such a thing as real life, for an artist? Were she and Adam quarreling? All these thoughts passed through Emily's head in a flash of discomfort. Adam turned his back on her and continued on up the hill, climbing faster and faster. She followed as best she could.

The first indication that something was seriously wrong came from Emily's ears. There was pressure in them, hammering. She paused in her upward course, clinging to a spindly tree. The hammering was her heart.

The hill was very steep at the place where she was holding on to the tree. Gravel slipped under her feet; loose pebbles launched themselves into space. She couldn't hear when they hit bottom. She turned and looked over her shoulder, wondering how she had gotten up here so high. The entire universe stretched away and away behind and below her, blue as dead men's eyes. If she took her hand off this tree she would fly into nothingness.

"Adam!" Emily's mouth was dry; her voice was a croak. "Adam!"

Above her, on the — it was a cliff, not a hill after all — on the cliff, Adam stopped climbing and looked down at her. "Come on, Emily, it's only a little way to the ledge."

"I think I'll stay here for a while."

"What do you mean, you think you'll stay here?"

"I'm having some kind of — the view is so nice, I thought I'd just stay right here and enjoy it." There was no spit in her mouth whatsoever.

"Do you want my help?" He began to scramble down the hill toward her. He steadied his hand on a rock but it came loose, came right off the side of the cliff and bounced quite near to her, missing her head by inches. "Sorry! Sorry. Are you okay?"

"Fine. It's all right. I'll just — I'm going to stay here for a minute or two. I'll meet you at the bottom of the hill."

"Give me your hand and we'll go down together." He descended a few more feet, dislodging more stones.

She imagined him prying her hand off the tree, forcing her to rely on his crazy incompetent self for guidance. The hammering of her heart was unbearable. She could scarcely breathe. "No. Leave me alone. Keep away from me."

"Emily!"

"I'm fine, darling, fine. Just let me stay here for a while. I can get down by myself. I'm — I'm enjoying the air."

"Suit yourself," he said. He went back down the hill toward the hotel. She was glad to see him go. Now it was just her and the sky and the little tree. She leaned her head against it and closed her eyes.

After a few minutes her heartbeat calmed, her breathing slowed, and she opened her eyes again. She could hear men's voices. Billy and Fred Parker were climbing the hill, arguing about something.

"I bet you five dollars it can't be done," Billy said.

"I bet you it can," Fred said. "They could build one of the towers in Washington Heights and the other one right there on that rocky outcropping. Then they could string some cables across and it's done."

"It's too far, brother." Billy emerged from the rocks and stood gazing back toward

Manhattan, followed by Fred.

"This is the twentieth century, brother. Engineering gets better all the time . . . Mrs. Weiss!"

"Hello, fellas," she said.

"You look like a baby bear, Mrs. Weiss," Billy said. "The way you're holding on to that sapling."

"Are you all right?" Fred said.

"Yes. I'm fine." Fred and Billy exchanged a nervous look. They seemed to think she might not be fine. "I'm fine, I am really. Where's Mr. Chalmers? Is he —"

"He was sober when we left him," Fred said.

"He didn't look like he was interested in drinking right then," Billy said. "He was talking to Miss Winningly. Are you sure you're all right?"

"Why wouldn't I be all right?"

"No reason."

"You fellas are awfully comfortable up here on the side of this cliff."

"Being up high isn't any different from being down low," Fred said. To emphasize his point he began a little dance, but stopped abruptly. He must have divined somehow that Emily was on the point of fainting.

"You're not really okay, are you?" Billy said.

94

"I tell you I'm fine."

"Anyway," Fred said, "like I was saying to Billy, it won't be too many years before they build a bridge over the river right here. What do you think?" He swept his hand out over the horizon. "Trolleys, cars, and trucks, all kinds of traffic, going from Manhattan to New Jersey and back again, right over this part of the river."

"Sounds like a good idea."

"If you'll let go of that tree for a minute I'll show you what I mean. You can sit here, put your feet right there. Take my hand. I'll help you. That's right. Take a deep breath, too. That's good. See how nice the air is up here?"

She closed her eyes and took two or three deep breaths. Her confidence began to return; the hammering in her ears subsided. "How long have you two been working on bridges?"

"Since before the disaster," Billy said.

"What disaster?"

"A railroad bridge in Canada collapsed while we were building it," Fred said. "Ninety-six men killed. Thirty-five of them Mohawks."

"Good heavens," Emily said.

"The women in the tribe were pretty up-set."

"I should think so. And yet you continue to work on bridges."

"They made us all split up after the disaster," Billy said. "The women. They didn't want us getting killed all at once. A lot of widows, a lot of mothers without sons. It was bad. But Fred and me still work together."

"It's a good trade, high steelwork," Fred said. "White people don't like it, for some reason."

"Except those old topmen who used to work on the sailing ships," Billy said. "They don't mind."

"Me, I don't understand being afraid of heights," Fred said. "Heights aren't anything. Look here, Mrs. Weiss, about ten inches below you is a good foothold. If you slide your right foot down you can feel it. You're all right, I've got your hand."

EIGHT

Foot by foot Fred Parker talked Emily down off the hill. She thanked him when they got to the road below and told the Indians not to mention it to anyone. Fred said, "Mention what?" So that was all right; her reputation was safe. Below them the ferry hooted; somewhere a crow called; life was back to normal.

Still, even on the flat ground in front of the Potts's front porch, Emily was keenly aware that Fort Lee was built more or less on the side of a cliff. Funny she hadn't noticed it before. There was no place to stand where her feet could be firmly planted on the earth, free from the danger of falling, or flying into space. This is crazy, she thought. I'm going nuts. I wonder whether I can get a drink in the hotel at this hour. But no, she had responsibilities; Adam had told her to hide the exposed film of the morning's shooting.

She found Mr. Johnson setting up his camera in the shadow of the stable. "Adam told me to get this morning's film from you and hide it."

"Take it," he said. "Hide it good. There's plenty more detectives where the first one came from. The old plaster has an unlimited supply. He might even send McCoy himself."

As if to prove the remark a stocky, bushy-haired man got off the trolley and looked around. A big mustache hid half his face, and yet somehow Emily thought he looked familiar. She turned her back to him, wrapped the can of film in the folds of her skirt, skulked to the cloakroom, and hid it under some hatboxes. Her nerves were in a state. A drink would be good. Maybe Mrs. Potts had a little something in the kitchen.

Suddenly a shriek came from the upper reaches of the hotel. It ran up Emily's spine like an electric shock.

Mr. Potts rushed down the stairs with his mouth open and his eyes rolling in different directions.

"What happened?" Emily said to him.

"It's an outrage," Mr. Potts said. "See here, Mrs. Weiss, you're going to have to control those actors of yours. This is a family hotel." His apple cheeks were like beets now, apoplectic.

"Why, what's the matter?"

"Mary Grace, our hired girl, discovered them in flagrante," Mr. Potts said.

"Flagrante?" Emily said. A neighboring town, perhaps, somewhere west of Coytesville. Adam had told them and told them not to stray too far from the set.

"In flagrante in the linen closet," Mr. Potts said. "I hope I need not say more."

Ah. That flagrante. "I'm shocked," Emily said. And strangely interested. The linen closet. A pile of cool, fresh sheets, smoothly ironed, delicately scented with lavender . . . yes, it had erotic possibilities. Maybe that was what she needed to help her calm down, fifteen or twenty minutes with Adam in the linen closet.

"Aside from the damage to the poor girl's morals, now she has to launder all those linens again. I hope you won't object, but I'm going to bill Melpomene Studios for her time."

Emily sighed. "It's only fair. I'll have a word with them. Who was it, if I may ask?"

The hotel keeper cleared his throat. Oh, God, not Adam.

"Miss Fay Winningly, and your" — It was! It was Adam! — "and your Mr. Chalmers, I believe he calls himself."

"I'm terribly sorry," Emily said, trying not to grin. "Please extend my deepest apologies to Mary Grace. Steps will be taken. The guilty will be punished. It will never happen again."

"I'll tell her, Mrs. Weiss," Mr. Potts said. "Unhappy girl. It's so hard to keep help nowadays."

"Thank you." Emily's heart was still hammering with alarm. But why should she think there was anything between Adam and the trashy Fay? Poor innocent, he was probably outside with Mr. Johnson and the extras, working himself to death setting up the next scene. She went upstairs to make sure the actresses were in costume.

Fay was locked in the bathroom, presumably putting herself to rights after her recent embarrassment and reapplying her cologne. Vera, all dressed and made-up, was pressing her side against the door frame and swinging her leg back and forth, keeping her knee straight and her toe pointed forward.

"What in the world are you doing, Vera?"

"Exercise."

"You swing your left leg for exercise?"

"Both legs. First left leg, then right leg." She turned around, leaned her left side against the frame of the door and began to swing her right leg now. The leg swung up to a remarkable height both in front and in back. "Is exercise to improve walking. Konstantin Sergeyevich tells us to do this every day. In Moscow Art Theater we do much work on our walking."

So. Vera's beautiful and enviable walk was a thing of art, a thing that she might teach to Emily. "Show me."

"Easily done," Vera said. "Is first placing right shoulder against frame of door. Is placing torso against frame of door also. Keeping back straight, keeping chin up, ears in line with shoulders, shoulders in line with hips, thus. Now, rising up on ball of right foot, keeping knees straight, is swinging left leg backward and forward as high as you can."

Emily tried it. "Not very high," she said.

"Not at first, no. But keep trying. Practice, practice, practice. Is giving you the free gait."

Fay Winningly, rolling her stocking up her leg, watched the two of them with an expression almost of contempt. "What would I want with a free gait?" she said.

"Looks good on film," Emily said.

"Also keeps feet healthy," Vera said. "Is good for your instrument, the plastic motion."

"What's she talking about?" Fay said. "Do

you know?"

"Sure," Emily said. "She's talking about Art." She swung her leg some more; her foot reached up a little higher, in the front anyway. "Is this the way?"

"Is good," Vera said. "Keep doing."

"Later," Emily said. "I have to see that the extras are properly costumed for the mob scene."

Mary Grace Canavan, the maid whose innocent sensibilities had been so sullied by the scene in the linen closet, was squinting at her reflection in the cloakroom mirror when Emily went downstairs to distribute the extras' costumes. "Is this good? I don't know whether I got the bow on the bonnet tied right."

"It's fine, Mary Grace. You're . . . you're the very picture of a prairie flower."

"You don't think I need more eye makeup?"

"Perhaps a little bit. Here." Emily took a brush and some grease-paint out of her bag and touched up the girl's eyes, even adding the red dot that was said to give one's gaze particular sparkle, although this touch was probably useless for film.

Mary Grace batted her eyelashes at her reflection. "Grand," she said. "You know, I never wore eye makeup in my life, before I was in your movies."

"There's a first time for everything, I guess."

"So do I look good enough?"

"Just about. You might take off the white lace collar. It's a little excessive."

"Here," she said, unpinning the offending article and handing it to Emily. "You know, if the movie company stays here I might become an actress full time."

"Really," Emily said.

"Mother won't like it, but Mother doesn't have to hear about it. She doesn't go to the movies."

"Doesn't your mother like movies?"

"She says they're sinful. That's nothing, I ought to tell her, you should see what goes on in hotel linen closets."

"Oh, about that, Mary Grace, I hope you don't —"

"She'll never find out. Mr. Potts won't tell on me. If he did he would have to say how it was his fault, how the nervous shock of finding people doing that in his linen closet drove me to it."

"Drove you to —"

"A life of sin as an actress."

"Dear me."

"I think being an actress would be grand."

"It has its ups and downs," Emily said.

"Let's go."

In the stable yard, almost everything was in readiness for the mob scene of *Lynching at Laramie.* The Wobblies had finished throwing the façade of the jail together, and somehow found time to put an artistic coat of paint on it, so that it looked weathered. Not a cloud marred the sky; the perfect light promised to continue for some time. Emily was gratified to see that Adam had gathered enough extras together to personate a convincing mob. Waiting to be pounded into the ground in front of the front steps of the jail was the iron spike attached to the big M for Melpomene.

Everyone in town was working in the movie — Mr. Potts, Joe from the livery stable, seven or eight housewives who lived down the street, Big Ed, all the Wobblies, of course, and even the Fort Lee police force, or three of them anyway. The policemen in their uniforms with the pot hats were inappropriate for the scene, of course, since they were meant to be part of a lawless mob. They would need flannel shirts and cloth caps.

"Could you put these on for me, please, Officer?" Emily said to the red-faced one with the chewing tobacco.

"Chief," he replied.

"I beg your pardon?"

"Don't call me officer, call me chief, little lady. I'm the police chief hereabouts. Francis X. Watson is the name."

And chiefing police is my game, Emily thought. How she detested being called "little lady." "I'm so sorry, Chief Watson. May I ask you and your men to take off your tunics and helmets, then, and put on these shirts and caps? We want you to pretend to be ordinary townspeople, for the movie."

"Yes, indeedy," Chief Watson said. "Here, boys." They hung their uniforms over the fence rail, out of range of the shot, which Mr. Johnson had defined with his customary rope, almost like half a baseball diamond.

Mr. Johnson and Adam were discussing where the players should go for the beginning of the shot. "Then we bring the crowd in from this side," Adam said. "Emily, can you round them all up for it? Oh, and get a white lace collar on that little maid. She disappears completely without something bright at her neck."

"Right, chief," Emily said. "But don't you think —"

Before she could argue her aesthetic point of view, the same stocky, mustachioed, bushy-haired man in the bowler hat and

105

topcoat who had gotten off the trolley before the linen closet business came and inserted himself between Emily and Adam, stepping on her foot. She might as well have been invisible to him. "Say, Mr. Weiss."

"What?" Adam said.

The back of the man's head, the place where the blackhead-ridden fat rolls met the edge of the auburn wig, spoke suddenly to Emily of Duffy.

"I have a property for you here," the man said. Yes, it was Duffy. "The movie rights will make you people a million dollars. I'm prepared to sell it for considerably less." He was carrying a fat manila envelope tied up with string.

"I'm not interested in properties right now," Adam said, narrowing his eyes. The false mustache and wig were not hard to spot.

Behind the detective's back, Emily made elaborate pointing gestures and mouthed, "Duffy." But the false mustache and wig were apparent even to Adam.

And apparently to everyone else on the lot, as it seemed. Big Ed Strawfield left off pounding the Melpomene M into the ground to look at him. Even Erno Berg was staring.

"However," Adam said, "if you'd like to

work as an extra in this picture, I can probably accommodate you. Emily, see about this man's wardrobe."

"An extra? Me? No, I've come here to give you this," he said, and he thrust the manila package into Adam's hand. "It's the story of my life, sir. I believe you'll find it fascinating, and I think you'll want to make it into a moving picture. After you read it we'll talk about money. And now I'll go and have a look at your movie camera, if you don't mind. Cameras interest me."

"Not a chance," Adam said. "Emily, our friend here is an extra. He is not to go near the camera. Have you got a flannel shirt for him?"

"I've got a humdinger," Emily said. She held out the very gaudiest of the shirts she was carrying over her arm.

"Oh, no. No, I couldn't," Duffy said. He took a step backward, bumping into Big Ed Strawfield, who was standing right behind him now, cracking his knuckles. "No." He cast his eyes here and there, but there was no avenue of escape.

"Mr. Weiss says you're an extra," Mr. Strawfield said. "Take off your coat and put on the shirt." And so he put on the shirt, handing his checkered topcoat to Emily.

"Come this way," Mr. Weiss said. He took

him by one arm while Big Ed took him by the other. Between the two of them they dragged Duffy up to the front of the crowd of extras and planted him between Chalmers and Chief Watson. Emily felt a tug on her sleeve.

Mary Grace. "Oh, good, here you are. Mr. Weiss wants me to put your lace collar back. Just stand still for a moment." Emily began to pin the collar. Adam put the megaphone to his lips and called for quiet.

"But where am I supposed to be?" Mary Grace said. "Ouch."

"Sorry," Emily said. "Go and stand over there with the rest of the crowd, outside the rope. Then when it's time for the crowd to come on scene, you go with them."

"How will I know?"

"Just keep your eyes on Mr. Strawfield."

Adam explained to the mob that he wanted them to tear down the jailhouse. It had to be done exactly right on the first take, because they couldn't afford the time to build it up again or the film to shoot it coming down. "Here's what happens in the scene. The outlaw is locked up in the jail. Erno is the sheriff. Fay is the outlaw's daughter. She comes to the jail and begs the sheriff for her father's life." Fay Winningly did some begging things with her arms, limbering up.

"But the lynch mob is on its way. Chalmers, Strawfield, you are at the front of the lynch mob. Strawfield, you follow Chalmers; the rest of you follow Strawfield. Stay out of the frame until I give the word. Watch the rope. Fay, you come to the jailhouse door when I tell you and beg Sheriff Erno for your father's life. Erno, when the scene begins you are standing in the doorway. You are resolute in the face of danger. Still, you understand that danger is all around." He took another step back. "Now. Roll the camera, Mr. Johnson!"

Emily looked over it all from a seat on the fence, a few feet away from the camera. She could see Erno Berg standing in the jailhouse doorway striking manly poses, and Fay Winningly's yellow curls. Outside of the frame the Wobblies flexed their arms and limbered their shoulders, while Mary Grace stared at Big Ed Strawfield the way a mouse watches a cat. Duffy's frowzy wig stuck up above the heads of the other extras. Adam waved his hands, put the megaphone to his lips and bellowed directions.

"Now!" Adam's amplified voice sounded strange, loud and thin at the same time. "Chalmers, you come into the frame, shaking your fist. Strawfield and the mob, come in behind him." The extras growled and muttered insults, getting into it. Some of the insults must have been in Finnish, for Erno Berg's face was suddenly contorted with rage. Never had Emily seen him show so much emotion.

"I like that look, Erno!" Adam shouted. "Could you direct it at Mr. Chalmers, please? You're glaring at that extra over there. You have nothing particular against him, right? Chalmers is your enemy."

"Erno!" Chalmers said. "Erno, look at me. Hold my gaze. You hate me. I'm your worst enemy." Erno looked at him. What a clever man Chalmers was, to be able to give Erno Berg acting lessons in the middle of a scene. What a useful man. If only he could stay sober and keep his hands off the girls.

"My worst enemy. You bet." The two men looked straight into each other's eyes, like two wild animals getting ready to fight. Erno softly muttered Finnish curses. The scene was working nicely.

"Now!" Adam shouted. "Rush the jailhouse, Chalmers! Follow him, crowd! Tear it down!" Chalmers lunged at the jailhouse door, pushing Erno to the ground. When the rest of them surged forward in a tangled mass, screaming, Emily feared that Erno might be trampled. Adam was with the crowd, rushing the jailhouse like the others. They were a real mob now. She could smell their sweat. People were elbowing one another and pushing to get to the front.

In the rising cloud of dust Emily could make out little of the action beyond the thrashing of plaid-clad arms and the shaking of fists. Duffy's gaudy shirt stood out for a moment and disappeared again. The sound of it all was terrifying, the growls, the grunts, the curses, the noise of wood ripping. Then the scenery was flying and Chalmers was chewing it, rising above the throng at one point to shout a few lines from "The Marseillaise." At last one of the Wobblies got a good grip on the front of the rickety structure and pulled. A huge section with a window in it fell forward, narrowly missing the extras.

"Aaand . . . cut!" Adam shouted. A stillness fell over the company. But someone couldn't stop screaming. It sounded like Mary Grace.

What in the world was the matter with the girl this time? Emily pushed her way through the crowd to see. There in the rubble of the jailhouse, his mustache half off, his wig all awry, his eyes blank and bulging, his torso pinned to the earth by the spike attached to the Melpomene trade-mark, was Duffy.

NINE

Emily gestured to Mr. Johnson to keep the camera rolling. The scene crackled with drama; surely they could use the footage for something later. The extras drew back from Duffy's body and formed a horrified circle.

Out of the crowd of extras stepped Francis X. Watson, the police chief. "Now, then, what have we here?" He bent over, hands on his thighs, and took a good look at the body. Emily distinctly heard him curse: "Goddamn son of a bitch."

Was Chief Watson cursing Duffy, or making a comment on things in general? Emily couldn't tell. He knelt down, examined the iron spike sticking out of Duffy's chest, and in a futile gesture felt his pulse. "Who did this?" Nobody spoke. "Does anyone here know this man?" He stared all around at the circle of faces until his gaze came to rest on Fay Winningly.

The actress squirmed, almost as though

with guilt. "It's Seamus Duffy, sir. A detective hired by Mr. Thomas Edison to get the goods on the movie company." She bit her finger.

"So it is," the police chief said. He peeled off the toupee and the remains of the mustache. "Does anyone know what he was doing here?"

"He came to stop Mr. Weiss from filming," Fay said. The whole company glared at her. "Well, he did," she said. "Didn't he? He came to ruin Mr. Weiss's business. Everyone said so."

"Mr. Weiss," the police chief said. He turned and looked at Adam. "Ruin, was it? That's a very strong motive for murder, wouldn't you say?"

"Don't be ridiculous," Adam said.

Fay burst into tears. "I didn't mean to tell him you did it," she sobbed. "I'm sorry, Mr. Weiss."

"What?" Adam said. Emily hoped Johnson was still cranking the camera. The people were all looking at Adam as if he were turning into a monster before their eyes. Those faces! What a shot! You couldn't hire them to play a scene like that, not for any money.

Of course they were fools, to listen to that silly woman. Chief Watson was the biggest fool of all of them.

Fay Winningly babbled on. "I know Mr. Duffy was going to expose you to Mr. Edison — I know that you and Mrs. Weiss stood to lose everything — but I didn't mean to say you killed him."

"No, and in fact I didn't kill him. Now see here, Miss Winningly —"

"He was so young," she sniveled.

"No, he wasn't," Emily said. "He was fifty if he was a day." Where did Fay get this stuff? Some play she had once had a minor part in, no doubt. Had she killed him herself, and was she carrying on like this to deflect attention? But, no, the trademark was too heavy and cumbersome for those delicate little hands to uproot from the frozen ground, still less to plunge into the breast of a bulky detective. Unless she was stronger than she looked.

"I'm afraid I'm going to have to place you under arrest, Mr. Weiss," the police chief said. "Come with me, please."

"Emily!" Adam cried.

"I'll get you a lawyer, Adam!" The crowd parted, and away went Chief Watson, frog-marching Adam to the lockup. The scene felt intensely unreal, even for someone in the movie business. Thankfully Mr. Johnson was still cranking away. He had many feet of horrified crowd scene by this time. "It's okay, Mr. Johnson, you can stop filming now," Emily said. "I mean to say, cut."

"I wanted to get everything on record. It might be evidence," Mr. Johnson murmured, glancing over his shoulder.

"What makes you say that?"

"The entire murder is right here on this reel in black and white. The killer will be in the frame." He blew out the alcohol lamp and started rewinding.

"Did you see anything?" Emily said.

"I didn't, no, but sometimes the camera picks things up."

A blow fell suddenly on Emily's shoulder. She started. It was only Ed Strawfield's heavy hand, meant to be comforting, she supposed. "Cheer up, Mrs. Weiss. The law hasn't got a thing on your husband. He'll be out in a week."

"A week! We don't have a week."

"And stop looking so sad. Duffy deserved to die. He was a Pinkerton detective and a dirty scab-lover and he had it coming."

Emily looked at the remains of Duffy, spread-eagled on the trampled brown grass of the meadow, with his false hair removed and the wreckage of the jailhouse façade littering his body, M for Melpomene protruding from his chest. How could anyone say he had it coming? And who cared whether he was a Pinkerton detective? Pinkertons. The most famous among a number of detective agencies who hired themselves out as private police forces in the lawless West. The Pinkerton agency had a branch office on Broadway a few doors down from the Schwartz Theatrical Agency. Emily used to pass their sign almost every day, a big eye with the words WE NEVER SLEEP. Just like Mr. Edison. She turned away with a shudder.

"Tell you what," Ed Strawfield said. "I'll put you in touch with my lawyer."

"Clarence Darrow? My soul. Who's going to pay him?"

"Don't worry about it. We'll find the money. There might even be a bounty on Duffy, a Pinkerton man and all. The Western Federation of Miners —"

"Why should anyone offer a bounty on Pinkerton men?" Emily shook her head. On the other hand, why not? The whole world was crazy.

"Class wars," Vera explained. Class wars in Fort Lee, New Jersey, Emily thought, this has such a cinematic quality; I should be taking notes. She looked again at the place where fell the hated Duffy, class warrior, Pinkerton man. Someone had taken away his body, leaving only a purple stain on the ground.

The extras lined up to be paid for their work in a high state of nerves, biting their lips, twisting their handkerchiefs, jiggling the change in their pockets. As Emily gave them their money she asked those who had been in the front ranks of the "mob" whether they had seen anything. They all said no, they had been too busy tearing down the false front of the jailhouse.

"Do you think Chief Watson wants us to stay in town?" Robert Chalmers said, sidling up to Fay Winningly and putting his arm around her. Fay shot him a sour look, took two steps away from him, and put her hand in the hand of Erno Berg. What's she playing, Emily thought, a game of musical men? "We could stay at the hotel, if you think we should," Chalmers persisted, addressing Emily this time. "I could rent a room."

Mrs. Potts was now at the front of the line of extras. "It's only fair to tell you, Mr. Chalmers, that you're no longer welcome in our hotel," she said. She slipped Melpomene's money into her apron pocket. "Nor Miss Winningly, neither. I think you both know why," and she went inside and slammed the door. Emily sighed. The last of the Wobblies took his pay and stood quietly with the others, waiting for Big Ed, who was waiting for Vera.

Vera lingered behind, nibbling her pearls. "So," she said. "Is the end of Melpomene Pictures?"

Surely not. "Of course it isn't," Emily said. "We'll be back in business as soon as this mess is cleaned up. Or before. Before the mess is cleaned up. Naturally it would be better if Mr. Weiss were out of jail, but I can direct movies almost as well as he can."

"Can you?" Chalmers said.

"Yes, yes. I've watched him work. There's nothing to it. And with such an excellent company of actors! It should be no problem for us to finish three more movies in" — she did a quick count on her fingers — "twelve days. I think it will be all right for you all to go home now. We know where to reach you. I'll contact you when we resume filming. It won't be long, a day or two depending on the weather." Indeed the clouds were gathering overhead again, slowly, the sort of blustery darkness that promised to last for at least a week.

The actors left. Mr. Johnson handed Emily the remaining film can. "Keep this under your coat," he whispered. "It might be safer for you if no one realizes you have it."

"Who would care if I have it, now that

Mr. Edison's detective is gone?"

"The killer."

"Oh. Oh, of course. I see your point."

"Unless you think it might really be Mr. Weiss who —"

"Certainly not. Do you know where the police station is?"

"Up the road about a hundred yards. You can't miss it."

Chief Watson told Emily there was no question of bail for a flighty movie person who might go anywhere as soon as he got free. He said Judge Birtch would hold a formal bail hearing as soon as he returned from his trip to Florida, but the police chief was sure the judge would agree with him. "You may speak with your husband for five minutes. Through the bars. I must be present the whole time, of course, to be sure you don't pass him any contraband."

Emily bit back a wisecrack about baking files in cakes and followed the chief into a short corridor that smelled of drunks and flop sweat. Adam sat hunched on his cot with his head bowed down, his hands hanging between his knees, almost as if the thrill of making movies had all gone out of him and left an inner core of nothing.

Emily wept, and tried to pretend she

wasn't weeping. To keep the film can from showing through her thin coat she shifted it awkwardly, thinking the chief might insist on taking it for evidence and then open the can and spoil the film.

"It's the end of Melpomene Pictures, Emily," Adam said.

"No, it isn't," Emily said. "I'll take care of things while we straighten this out. I can't understand what Fay was thinking. Why did she say those things?"

"I could strangle her," Adam said. "Cheerfully. If I had my hands around her neck right now — !"

"Hush," Emily said.

"No, sweetheart, Melpomene is doomed. Thomas Edison has the last laugh on us. But don't worry. If I get out of this I can always go back to work at Horn and Hardart."

"You'll do no such thing. We have almost two weeks to finish the last three pictures. Even if it rains half the time, that should be plenty. I can direct them myself."

"Do you think so?"

"Certainly. Mr. Johnson can help me set up the shots, and Robert Chalmers can give me tips on getting the actors to emote in front of the camera. He's quite good at that,

I think, except with Vera, who has her own
—"

"... Method. You may be right. I hope so,
sweetheart. Yes. I have every confidence in
you." He didn't sound as if that were really
true. Just the same she told him she loved
him.

"Have you done anything about a lawyer?"
he said.

"We're getting Clarence Darrow," she
said.

"Ah." He glanced at Chief Watson. Watson's face showed nothing. The name of
Clarence Darrow did not intimidate him.

"Mr. Darrow will be here soon," Emily
said. Still no reaction from Watson. Perhaps
he had never heard of Clarence Darrow. Or
he wasn't listening. "Soon. In the meantime
I want you to be brave until I find out who
the real murderer is. Or murderess. For
example, Fay Winningly could have been
accusing you to take attention away from
herself. I believe she's much stronger than
she looks. If she used both hands, she could
have —"

Chief Watson was listening after all. He
puffed up like a toad. "You'd best let it
alone, little lady. The police are perfectly
capable of taking care of this matter."

"No, they're not," Emily said. "You put

my husband in jail. A completely innocent man."

"Time's up. Let's go."

"It isn't, either. I have another minute and a half."

"Out."

"Good-bye, Adam, my darling," she said. "I'll be back tomorrow."

Thick darkness enveloped Fort Lee as Emily dragged herself back to the hotel. She was tempted to check in and spend the night in one of the hotel's clammy rooms. Mr. and Mrs. Potts would probably let her, since she wasn't the one who misbehaved in the linen closet, but in spite of her fatigue she wanted to get to the darkroom in the Knickerbocker and process the day's work. The first can of film would bring Melpomene one picture closer to fulfilling its contractual obligations. The second can, when it was developed, might well reveal Duffy's killer and get Adam out of jail.

Between the police station and the hotel the amber glow of electric lights shone out of the windows of people's houses. Sometimes the light spilled onto the slate sidewalk, whose surface was irregular where tree roots had heaved the slates. Emily had to watch her step to keep from tripping. She glanced up through a lighted window and saw a family gathered around their dinner table, the father sharpening his carving knife, the children waiting with napkins tied around their necks, one little fellow bowing his head and folding his hands in prayer.

Emily tried to picture Adam at the head of his own table, master of his own house, surrounded by pious children, preparing to carve a roast of beef. If Melpomene failed to deliver four pictures to Howie Kazanow by the required date, there would be no house; if Emily failed to discover Duffy's real killer there would be no children and no Adam, for they would take him to Trenton and electrocute him in Mr. Edison's horrible new chair.

The Potts Hotel loomed up as a dark mass against the skyline. Mr. Potts hadn't any guests at all tonight, evidently, and was keeping the lights in the front of the place turned off as an economy measure. But something large was waiting in the dark on the top step of the porch. As Emily approached she thought she saw a hulking beast with malevolent burning eyes.

TEN

The menace on the steps of the Potts Hotel shifted slightly, and then its burning eyes bounced off in two different directions. Cigarettes. Two people were sitting in the dark, smoking.

Emily had forgotten all about Fred and Billy.

"We thought you might like somebody to see you safe to the ferry," Fred said.

"Indeed I would."

"We'll just go down to the ferry landing with you. We're staying here in Jersey," Fred said.

"Fred found a good boardinghouse in Coytesville this afternoon," Billy said.

"The lady of the house is a Seneca," Fred said. "She makes really good fried bread."

"Did either of you see what happened today?"

"We heard about it," Billy said.

"We were in Coytesville," Fred said, "looking at the boardinghouse."

"Mr. Weiss said he didn't want us in that scene," Billy said. "Our characters are supposed to appear later in the film and he thought the audience might recognize us."

How carefully Adam had planned this picture, shifting the cast members here and there. Now Emily herself would have to do all of that, at least until Adam was free. She picked up the clothes and the other can of film from the cloakroom and started down the cliff road in the bitter wind, with an Indian boy on either side of her. The trolley was nowhere in sight. Billy was shivering.

"Billy, take this woolen shirt and put it on over your other clothes. You'll catch your death of cold. Or, better, here's a topcoat." A moment passed before she remembered whose topcoat it had been.

"Thanks, Mrs. Weiss. I'll give it back tomorrow."

"Keep it. It was Mr. Duffy's. He won't need it anymore."

"It's kind of big on me, but it's good and warm. Wait a minute, here's something, might be his wallet. You better take this, Mrs. Weiss."

It was indeed a wallet, though it was too dark to see what was in it. Plainly her duty was to turn back up the hill and give the wallet, unexamined, to the scornful, dense, and stupid Chief Watson. And miss the last ferry. But Emily had higher duties.

The processed film of the riot scene took hours to dry, time enough for Emily to wash and dry her hair and braid it for the night, read all her magazines twice, and practice the Moscow Art Theater leg-swinging exercise until she could get her right foot, at least, higher than her waist. By three o'clock in the morning the positive print was dry enough to run through the projector.

Here was a camera's-eye view of the murder, and it showed exactly what Johnson said he saw, which was nothing. Nothing unexpected, that is. As Emily slowly cranked the projector all she could see was a mass of heaving flannel-clad backs. Then the distinctive plaid of Duffy's shirt appeared in the frame.

And there was the great big M for Melpomene, rising in the air. She stopped the projector and squinted at the frozen picture.

Many recognizable heads were close to Duffy's head. Fay. Erno. Robert Chalmers. Ed Strawfield. Two of his Wobblies.

Adam.

All of their faces, however, were turned upward, not toward the doomed detective.

The façade of the jail was getting ready to collapse, and anyone with sense prepared to protect himself against falling debris. Maybe the big M fell on Duffy by accident. No, that wasn't possible. Someone had to pull the iron spike out of the ground.

Emily advanced the film another frame. The M was coming down, but so was the scenery, and the scrambling actors were little more than a blur on the makeshift screen. In the next frame the blurring was worse. So much for Emily's dream of carrying the film and projector to the Fort Lee police station and using it to exonerate Adam. From what she could see on the film, Adam could very easily be guilty.

Almost in her sleep she rewound the film. In the morning she would take the first completed moving picture to the processor for duplication, so that when Adam got free he would at least not be facing ruin.

Bessie, the well-bribed chambermaid, had made the bed up that day with clean sheets and pillowcases. All traces of Adam were gone; still Emily held his pillow while she drifted into the land of nightmare. Electric light from the unsleeping city leaked in the windows and turned into sunlight on the cliffs at Fort Lee. The hiss and clink of the steam radiator became the sound of Mr.

Johnson's camera. She saw Adam's face. She saw his face smiling as he muscled the reluctant Duffy up to the front of the crowd of extras, where the action was about to take place.

Duffy's wallet! The thought of that item brought Emily wide awake, sitting bolt upright in bed, as the gray light of dawn came in around the window blinds. Someone had killed the detective for a reason, and since it wasn't Adam killing him to preserve Melpomene Pictures, then it was someone else, for some other reason that could only be understood by finding out who he was and who he had offended. The wallet would hold clues to who he was, other than a clumsy practitioner of disguise (couldn't call him a master, she had never seen a more fake-looking mustache in her whole career on the stage), servant of the evil Thomas Edison, Pinkerton agent, and dirty scab-lover. Who had called him a Pinkerton man? Strawfield. What made Strawfield say that? Did he know him?

The wallet was still in her coat pocket. She spread the contents out on the bed. Fifty-seven dollars in fives and ones. Membership in the East Side Athletic Club. Ticket to the 1909 New York Policeman's

Ball. Standard identification card that must have come with the wallet. The ID card was pathetic, in its way; Duffy had filled in his name, address, and telephone number in a square stubby hand, but the line next to "Notify in Case of Emergency" he had left blank. The man had no one who cared what happened to him.

But, his address. The place where he lived would be bristling with clues to the sort of life he led. If Emily could get a crack at it before the police, she might find out who had a reason to kill him.

Besides Adam.

To save her husband, Emily must go to this address and search Duffy's things. Of course she couldn't just walk in there, the wife of the chief suspect in Duffy's murder. She put some stage makeup, a brightly flowered gypsy shawl, and a black Indian princess wig into her bag, tucked the completed film in its can under her arm, and set forth.

It was raining outside, but the subway door in the lower floor of the Knickerbocker would enable Emily to travel the length of Manhattan right from the hotel without ever getting her feet wet. The new modern subway would take her first to the film processor and then to the lair of the dead detective to do some detective work of her own. Like a fish entering some great river she slipped through the door and into the crush of strangers thronging Times Square Station.

Duffy's address proved to be that of a boardinghouse whose door was answered by a formidable Irishwoman in a house dress. This person would never be able to identify Emily, since the disguise she had hastily donned in a nearby alley (a black wig, a wildly patterned shawl, and a hideous collodian scar) made her look quite unlike herself, but rather like some gypsy who had dyed her hair and fallen into a fire.

"I'd like to see Seamus Duffy," Emily mumbled through twisted lips. "I'm his sister." The scar was so ugly that the woman had to avert her gaze.

"He's not at home," the woman said. "Hasn't been home all night. Fact is, I haven't seen him since breakfast yesterday."

Emily pulled her gaudy shawl more tightly around herself. "He promised to meet me here this morning," she said. "May I wait for him in his room?"

"I dunno," the woman said. "Mr. Duffy doesn't like me to let people into his room."

"But I've come so far, and it's so cold out

here," Emily said. "Oh! Oooh . . ." She swayed, and leaned against the door frame. The woman put her knuckles to her mouth and darted a glance up and down the street at the half-closed blinds of the neighbors. Emily thought, she's afraid I'll cause a scandal. That's good. I'll pretend I'm pregnant. She clutched her stomach and moaned again. "Just for a minute or two. Then if he doesn't come for me, I'll . . . I'll be on my way. . . ."

"I guess it'll be all right," the woman said, and opened the door for her to come in out of the sight of the neighbors. "Would you like anything? A cup of tea?"

"No, thank you," Emily said. "If I could just sit down for a little while, among dear Seamus's things." She put a trembling hand to her hair, thinking, I hope it isn't coming loose.

"It's the second floor back, then," the woman said. Emily tottered up the stairs and down the hall to her "brother's" room, closed the door behind her, and shot the bolt.

The late Seamus Duffy had lived in a hell of old cigar butts and stale beer, but he kept a tidy desk. Emily saved the desk for last. In his wardrobe hung the checkered suit he had worn on the dock the day she first saw him. The pockets were empty, as were the pockets of the three pairs of assorted pants hanging next to it. On the floor of the wardrobe were two pairs of shoes, one in oxblood, well-shined, with buttons up the side, and one pair of scuffed brogans suitable for a disguise as a vagrant. A hatbox held a tweed cap, his second-best derby, the first best having been on his head when he died, and a number of wigs.

On Duffy's windowsill was a sad little potted plant with two cigar butts in its saucer. What a stench. Nothing was buried in the dirt of the pot except the plant's own unhealthy roots. On his dressing table were a shaving kit, military brushes, and a comb. In the drawer was the usual assortment of men's knickknacks, cuff links, matches, and the like. Emily glanced in the mirror and started violently; the makeup with the collodian scar was hastily done, but too well, and the wig was truly hideous. Let me remember this sight, she thought, if ever I am tempted to dye my hair black. She closed the dressing-table drawer again. Duffy's sock drawer held socks and garters; in his underwear drawer he kept his underwear, singlets, drawers, and union suits; under his pillow was a large shiny revolver, fully loaded, and under his bed was a smelly chamber pot. Ugh.

Now for the desk.

Lying right out in plain sight on top of the otherwise neat desk, a simple fumed-oak affair with two drawers, one deep and one shallow, was a cream-colored envelope addressed in pica typewriting to Mr. Seamus Duffy. The return address engraved on the back was none other than the New York office of the Pinkerton National Detective Agency. Aha! So he did work for the Pinkertons. The envelope had been hastily opened already, the opening torn and ragged. She pulled out the letter inside and unfolded it. The letter was typed on Pinkerton letterhead and dated the previous week.

Dear Mr. Duffy:

It has come to our attention that you continue to persist in your intention to publish your memoirs. Once again we must remind you of your duly sworn and notarized oath never to make public anything you did or heard of while you were a Pinkerton agent. Should you choose to break this oath, the civil penalties will be severe, and there may be criminal charges as well.

We urge you to destroy these memoirs, or better yet to turn them over to the nearest Pinkerton office, where we will see that they never come into the light of day. A sworn oath is a serious matter, Mr. Duffy. Think well upon what you are doing. Expect to hear from our lawyers, Alford, Alford and Watts, in regard to this matter. Until that time believe me to be

Your obedient servant,
Burton Haslemere
Supervising Agent

So Duffy had been a Pinkerton agent once, and had seen and done things that would be embarrassing to the Pinkerton agency if they were ever made public. This was surely a clue. The Pinkertons killed him, then, infiltrating the movie set somehow among the townspeople and Wobblies. Where were these memoirs? Not in the shallow drawer; nothing was there but pencils, a broken fountain pen, a jar of ink, two sticks of sealing wax, a quantity of rotted rubber bands, a pack of business cards, all bearing different names and businesses, and a round, flat, gray, gritty ink eraser attached to a black brush for whisking the paper crumbs.

She pulled out the deep drawer and riffled through the file folders. Duffy kept his business accounts in a ledger in the front of the drawer. This was followed by a section labeled "Case Notes," file after file on his individual cases. A busy fella was our Duffy. Here was a file labeled "Melpomene." She pulled that one out and tucked it in her shawl. After "Case Notes" came another section full of files, "Items of Interest." Way in the back was a capacious dog-eared folder labeled "Memoirs." It was empty.

A gentle tap sounded on the door.

Emily soundlessly straightened the desk. "Yes?" she called.

"Miss Duffy, may I come in?" It was the landlady.

"Certainly," Emily said. She put the Melpomene file under the pillow with Duffy's gun and wrapped the shawl around herself before she opened the door. The landlady carried a hot cup of tea and a newspaper.

"I've some bad news for you, dear," the landlady said. "You'll want to sit down. Take this." Emily lowered herself into the chair in front of Duffy's dressing table. There was gin in the brutally strong cup of tea. She drank it down. "I don't know how to break this to you gently. Your brother's dead, murdered over in Fort Lee, New Jersey. Some of them wicked movie people done him in."

"Oh, no," Emily cried, and buried her face

in her hands. "My poor Seamus." A bit of collodian stuck to her thumb. If I pull it away the scar will come with it, she thought, right here in front of this woman.

"Here's the story in this morning's *Post,*" the landlady said. Emily put out the hand that wasn't glued to her face and took the newspaper. "I'm so sorry for your trouble," she went on. "First the injury to your face and now this. If you'll excuse my bringing it up."

"It's all right," Emily said, shifting her grip. Oh, horrors, now she had the stuff stuck in her hair. "I'd like to be alone for a minute, if you don't mind."

"Whatever you say." The landlady gave her a sudden shrewd look. Emily thought, She suspects something. I'd better be quick. The minute the door closed behind the landlady Emily peeled her hand away from her face and wig and dived into the desk drawer. What was it that Duffy considered to be items of interest?

His blackmail files.

Many strange names, but then here was Fay Winningly. Robert Montmorency. Chief Francis X. Watson.

Outside she heard footsteps on the stairs, and the landlady's voice: "She's up this way, Officer Feeny, a very fishy one and that I can tell you."

Emily threw the bolt on the door, rushed to the window and pushed aside the fly-blown window shade. Duffy's unhappy potted plant fell to the floor with a crash. Outside the window a rickety iron fire escape offered a way down to the street. She grabbed up all of Duffy's items of interest files that she thought might be of interest to her personally, plus the Melpomene report under the pillow, lingered for a second over the gun, and ended by taking that too, although it was very heavy.

The landlady and the policeman began to shout at her and pound on Duffy's door. Emily tried to raise the window sash. It came banging down; the sash weight ropes were broken. She raised it again and propped it up with a stick she found behind the windowsill. A gust of wind carried the cold rain in the window. Twenty feet below was the garbage-strewn alley that led to the street and freedom. Twenty measly feet. She had only to climb down and run away. A simple matter.

She put her leg over the windowsill, placed her foot on the iron platform, tried her weight on it. The platform wobbled a little. Bolts held the whole works to the brick wall of the building, and they were rusted, wiggly, and loose. Yes, the bolts were almost certain to let go. The second she was out on the platform they would pull out of the wall entirely and let her fall. She saw herself falling, crashing, lying dead in a tangle of rusted iron and garbage.

The paving below slowly began to revolve.

The landlady and the policeman were shouting at each other now; he wanted to batter the door down, but it was the landlady's door and she wished to spare it. "Go outside and around, you ignorant spalpeen," the landlady bellowed. "Open it from the inside."

"Get a locksmith, you old hairpin."

"I'm tellin' you there's a criminal in there, all in disguise, stealing Seamus Duffy's things."

"Then stand aside, woman, while I force the door."

Emily straddled the windowsill, her skirt hiked up to her knees, no spit in her mouth once again. Her legs were made of jelly. She was twenty-five years old, in the full vigor of her youth, and never in her life before had her physical powers failed her in this way. She thought desperately, What's different? I'm old. I'm married. It must be like Samson and his hair. The alley yawned before her like some awful abyss. Terror was up to

139

her neck and rising. She could not, could not climb over that windowsill.

ELEVEN

"Mr. Weiss, your lawyer is here to see you."

Adam looked up from the stained floor, at which he had been staring in intense concentration for several hours, to behold the resplendently caparisoned figure of Howie Kazanow. His feet twinkled in white spats, his hands gleamed in kidskin gloves, his tie sparkled with a four-carat zircon stickpin, and all the rest of him glittered with tailoring of such fine (if gaudy) quality that he might already be spending Adam's money.

"I'd like a moment alone with my client, please," Kazanow murmured to Chief Watson. The policeman bowed deferentially and left.

"You don't look to me like Clarence Darrow," Adam said.

"And you don't look to me like a successful movie producer. What the hell are you doing in jail, Adam? Who's making the pictures you owe me?"

"Melpomene Studios is making the pictures. Production is right on schedule. Never fear. I do, however, seem to need a lawyer. Have you come here to represent me, or to gloat?"

"I don't do trial work. Did you kill this guy, Adam?"

"No."

"You just stick to that story. You'll be fine."

"Okay, then, to what do I owe the pleasure? Are you here to bail me out?"

"You look terrible, Adam. Don't they let you shave?"

"If I had a razor right now I would cut one of our throats."

"Have a cigar," Howie said. Adam took it, despising himself. "I'm here to help you. Under the terms of our contract you forfeit everything if I don't have four movies in hand a week from next Tuesday." Howie lit Adam's cigar, a good Havana, and then his own. "I'm willing to give you a break. You can have a two-week extension, and it will only cost you two thirds. I'm a reasonable man, Adam; I don't want to ruin you, a newlywed and all that." He withdrew an envelope from an inner pocket of his jacket, took out some papers, and handed them to Adam, together with a gold-plated fountain pen.

"Two thirds of what?" Adam said. "Two thirds of the profits, or two thirds of what I have invested in Melpomene?"

"Both. Adam, I'm not in business for my health here. Our partnership involves considerable risk to me."

"Nice hat."

"Thanks. I bought it in Newport."

"They have hat stores in Newport?"

"You'd be surprised."

"I tell you what, Howie." Adam handed back the pen and the papers. "Why don't you take a good dump in that hat, pull it over your ears, and see what it does for your complexion."

"I'm sorry you feel that way, Adam. Sorry for you. I'm afraid you're going to live to regret it."

Trapped in Duffy's window, Emily was forced to surrender to her strange new terror of heights. She was searching her mind for a way out that didn't involve climbing when she heard the policeman bellow at the landlady, "All right then, missus! I'm going around!" The banging on the door stopped abruptly. Only the pounding in her ears remained. She pulled her foot back in. Soon the policeman would be coming up the fire escape.

If she couldn't climb down she couldn't. That's all there was to it. She would have to find some other means of getting out of this. Perhaps by throwing a handful of plant pot dirt out onto the fire escape platform she could create a false trail, hide in the room somewhere, and then . . . She threw the dirt, backed into the wardrobe next to Duffy's checkered suit, and pulled the door shut in front of herself with a soft click.

After a minute her breath began to come back. She shifted her weight. Her skirt was caught in the wardrobe door, sticking out into the room. She opened the door and pulled it all the way in.

The fire escape began to shudder and clang. The wardrobe door stubbornly refused to latch now. She held it shut with her fingernails, trying to keep her hand from shaking, as the policeman climbed over the windowsill. The hammering of her heart sounded louder than his footsteps crossing the room. Then he pulled back the bolt on the door between Duffy's room and the hall. The landlady came in, making outraged huffing noises.

"She's gone, Mrs. O'Rourke," the policeman said. "She left a trail of dirt all over the fire escape and got away."

"Huh. If you'd been a little quicker on

your pins you'd have had her."

"Look around, see if she stole anything," he said.

"I will."

"Check the closet, why don't you."

Emily braced herself. If necessary she would stick Duffy's gun in their faces and back herself down the stairs like a movie outlaw. Footsteps approached the wardrobe. She groped for the gun.

"No, Officer Feeny, the truth is I can't be bothered. I have no idea what the man had that would be worth stealing, and I wouldn't know what was missing. And as for himself, he's gone, poor soul. Did you hear what happened? Them movie people done him in."

They went away, still talking. The door banged shut. Emily waited a long time before she dared to stir hand or foot. A day and a half went by, or so it seemed; when she heard no further sounds, she ventured with stiff knees out of the wardrobe, into the empty room, and then into the empty hall.

She tiptoed down the stairs into a strong smell of cabbage and the sound of pots and pans banging. The landlady must have been occupied with preparing the noon meal. Then someone spoke in a deep, urgent voice, not the old pensioner in the morris chair in the parlor, reading a newspaper with his back toward her, but one of the two men standing in the archway between the parlor and the dining room. With an electric thrill Emily recognized the backs of the Great Dane and the bull terrier.

"I'm telling you, Mrs. O'Rourke, I'm Seamus Duffy's brother Mickey," the Great Dane said. "You've got to let me into his room to take care of his final arrangements."

"And I'm Sean," said the bull terrier. "His other brother. Don't tell me he never mentioned us."

"Yerra," said Mrs. O'Rourke. "You can tell that story to Officer Feeny, for I'm after calling him this minute. It will do you no good to go through your so-called brother's things in any case, for your so-called sister has already beat you to it. So there, you crooks. Bad luck to you and get out of my boardinghouse."

Emily was out the front door and running down the rainy street before the last words of this speech had left the landlady's mouth. Not until she had gained the safety of her room at the Knickerbocker did she stop to get her breath.

She spread the stolen file folders out on the bed. Some were fatter than others, all rather grubby with fingerprints. Duffy must have seldom washed his hands. Each folder bore a tab on the top with someone's name written on it, presumably the blackmailee. Most interesting to Emily was the thinnest, the file labeled Fay Winningly, first of all because Emily didn't like Fay, but mostly because she was on fire to learn what secrets Fay could conceivably have wanted to conceal. Everyone knew Fay went to bed with any man who would give her the smallest encouragement. You couldn't blackmail a person like that.

A single manila envelope was all that the file folder contained. Emily opened the envelope. In it was a photograph. She shook it out into her hand. Her heart was pounding. It might be a picture of Fay in bed with Adam. In that case Emily would be forced to take Duffy's gun and go shoot the miserable girl.

But, no, it was a photograph of a document with an official seal. Someone's birth certificate.

Not blackmail files, then, but other items of interest. One of the files had Chief Watson's name on it. Nothing in that file but a small notebook, the pages ledger-ruled, with penciled dates, initials, and figures in a spidery hand. Casting aside two files with names on them of people she had never heard of, Emily opened Robert Montmorency's folder. A picture of him sleeping. Incriminating? No, he was alone. What possible use — ? Then she noticed the pipe dangling from his fist, the crude bunk bed he occupied with its greasy ticking pallet, the drooping shoe on the foot of the man in the bunk above him, and the long-fingernailed hand in the brocaded sleeve projecting into the picture, holding a smoking clay pipe. A picture of Broadway actor Robert Montmorency passed out cold in a Chinese opium den.

Very well, these had to be blackmail files. The chief's little notebook, then, was probably a running record of municipal graft. Emily understood all about these things from reading *McClure's Magazine.*

She looked again at the photograph of the birth certificate in Fay's file. Fay Muggins. Not a good stage name; no wonder she had changed it. But surely no disgrace. Was she perhaps illegitimate? No. Her mother and father were listed as married to each other. Born in Ames, Iowa. No disgrace there, either. But the date on this birth certificate, if it became generally known, would surely cause serious damage to Fay's career: October 22, 1879.

Little Fay Winningly was thirty years old, and still making her living playing adolescent schoolgirls. Would she kill to keep her real age a secret? Many another actress would.

Emily turned to the file labeled Melpomene, not a blackmail file, at least not that she knew of, but a record of Duffy's activities on behalf of his client, Thomas Edison. It held a few reports meant to be sent to Mr. Edison, or, more likely, copies of reports that had already been sent to him, written in ink in Duffy's square and stubby handwriting. There is something organic and alive in a person's handwriting, almost as much as in the sound of his voice. Seeing those bold strokes reminded Emily of the shape of Duffy's hands, and for the first time she realized in her viscera that he was dead. Even though she didn't like him, even though he died working actively against her interests, the man's death saddened her.

Here in the Melpomene file was a penciled note he wrote to himself, dated yesterday.

Received telephone message from F.W.
— filming to resume today.
If today's investigation unsuccessful will hire another operative.

F.W.? Was Fay Winningly selling out her own employers to keep Duffy from revealing her age? If so, no wonder she had to kill him. When Melpomene folded Fay herself would be out of yet another job.

Emily made herself presentable, had lunch at a restaurant near the ferry slip, and ventured across the river to Fort Lee. Giving Adam a progress report would be hard, with the chief of police standing right at her shoulder, but she knew he would want to be kept up-to-date on the latest developments. As she sat on the cold slats of the green-painted ferry bench she thought of writing everything down, passing Adam the note in secret, whispering to him that he was to eat it after he read it. But, no. There were too many ways for such a plan to go awry. Adam's appetite, for instance, was very light these days.

What was wanted was a distraction, she decided, as she went up the steps, through the glass door, and into the police chief's office. "Chief Watson, I have something for you. This is Mr. Duffy's wallet. It turned up among the props when I went to straighten them out this morning."

"Why, thank you, Mrs. Weiss."

"Can I see my husband now?"

"I think it will be all right. Go ahead. I'll be right along." She turned to leave the chief's office. Reflected in the glass of his office door she thought she saw him lifting the greenbacks out of Duffy's wallet. Of course, she could have been mistaken; the glass was wavy, and the light was bad.

Adam sat on the cot behind bars, looking, if anything, worse than he had the day before.

They touched fingertips through the bars. "Darling, are you eating anything? You look terrible."

"The food isn't very interesting here."

A newspaper lay open beside him. "At least you have something to read," she said.

"The chief gave it to me. Nice guy, the chief." Emily noticed the headline: DEATH BY ELECTRIC CHAIR NOT PAINLESS, DOCTORS ARGUE. FLESH CHARS, BLOOD SQUIRTS FROM SKIN OF CONDEMNED MAN. The illustration was a line drawing of a straight wooden armchair with straps, wires, a leather blindfold, and some kind of tin cap attached to it. No dead murderers were pictured.

"Don't pay any attention to that, Adam. What would you like to eat? I'll get Mrs. Potts to make you up some supper and bring it over." He didn't reply. She leaned closer and spoke very softly. "I think Fay Winningly killed Duffy. He was blackmailing her."

Adam snickered.

"No, really. He was blackmailing half of Fort Lee. Including" — she dropped her voice to a whisper — "Chief Watson. He'll be in here in a second. Listen. You know that manuscript that Duffy gave you yesterday? I need it. Do you know where you left it?"

"Why? It was only a pretext for Duffy to get on the set."

"No, I think it was his actual memoirs. There might be something in it that would tell us who would want to kill him. Besides Fay."

"Fay didn't murder Duffy. That's a ridiculous idea."

"Try to think, Adam."

Adam visibly tried to think, frowning, rubbing his hair. "I didn't have it on me when I was arrested. The package was too big to put in my pocket."

"And so . . ."

"I put it down."

"You put it down in the stable yard?"

"Wherever it was that I was standing. Somewhere out of the frame of the shot we were filming."

"By the fence?"

"Yes. That would be it. By the fence."

"In the rain."

"It wasn't raining yesterday." Chief Watson came shuffling into the corridor and cleared his throat meaningfully. Adam said, "Listen, Emily, if it doesn't rain tomorrow you have to call Johnson and the actors and get busy. Finish the second Western. Start on the comedy. We only have eleven days left. Forget this foolishness about Fay. Forget looking for Duffy's killer. Finish these pictures. Then we'll have money for a good defense. Didn't you tell me that Big Ed Strawfield was getting Clarence Darrow for us?"

"Adam, somebody other than you killed that man," she said. "If I can I'm going to find out who it was."

"But not right now. Not when our whole future together depends on finishing these moving pictures."

"I'd sooner see you working in Horn and Hardart than sizzling in Mr. Edison's electric chair."

"Emily, you have to trust me."

How could she trust him? He had made of their lives a complete mess. Now here he sat, crumpled like a discarded page of scenario, giving her what she knew was bad advice. She opened her mouth to argue with him, and thought better of it; he was helpless in there; she had a horrible feeling he was going to start weeping. "I'm sorry, Adam. I'm sorry. I'll get right on it. We'll finish the picture tomorrow." He didn't answer. Chief Watson took her by the arm and made her leave.

Mrs. Potts agreed to take some supper over to the jail for Adam, something wholesome and comforting. She hadn't seen Duffy's manuscript anywhere. "I'll look around for it," she said.

"Thanks. I'll check the stable yard," Emily said. She went outside and searched beside the fence, under the bushes, and in the muddy places. She looked through the hay in the stable while the smelly horse nickered and stamped. The manuscript was nowhere to be found.

Back in New York Emily gathered a pocketful of nickels and telephoned Johnson and all the actors from the pay phone in the lobby of the Knickerbocker, telling them if the sun was out the next morning they were to meet at the ferry slip. Everyone agreed to be there except Fay Winningly.

"I'm leaving Melpomene Studios," Fay said.

"Oh, please don't do that, Miss Winningly."

"I'm sorry, Mrs. Weiss, but I've had an offer from American Biograph. They're making a feature-length film called *Jane White's School Days* and they've offered me the starring role. Mr. D. W. Griffith is directing."

"Isn't there some way you could handle both parts?"

"I'm afraid not. Biograph is relocating their studios to California. The sun shines all the time there, you know."

"So you're quitting in the middle of our movie."

A long sigh. "Fort Lee is a very painful place for me now, Mrs. Weiss. I'm sure you understand."

Maybe Emily did understand. If Fay had killed Seamus Duffy, the farther away she got from Fort Lee the safer she would feel.

Could Vera take Fay's place in a blond wig? No. *Lynching at Laramie* was ruined, after all their work and grief, unless Fay's character could be somehow . . .

"I'm sorry I can't persuade you to stay, Miss Winningly. Good luck with Biograph," Emily said. "I wish you every success." The scenes in *Lynching at Laramie* that she and

Adam had written for Fay flashed in her mind's eye. Not one of them was crucial to the movie's success, not if they changed the plot slightly.

For instance, not if Fay's character was said to have been killed in the lynching scene. In that case one of the extras could stretch out under a blanket and pretend to be dead Fay while Erno grieved over her body. Erno, thirsting for revenge. Vera weeping. It might even make a better picture.

The small matter of bringing Fay to justice for Duffy's murder could wait until later, when Emily was able to find something solid against her. California was not out of reach of the long arm of the law.

TWELVE

"Good morning, people. I'm glad to see you all here this morning. As you know this is a critical time for Melpomene Moving Picture Studios, but if we all pull together we'll be able to finish our pictures before the deadline, which is now ten days away, and when that happens there'll be bonuses for every one of you."

The cast and crew of Melpomene Moving Pictures, gathered in the stable yard of the Potts Hotel to finish *Lynching at Laramie,* greeted Emily's announcement with a feeble cheer. Some were shivering, and all were breathing in visible puffs. They took turns warming themselves at the steel fire barrel. A large blue and white spatterware coffeepot sat on a grate over the fire, filled with coffee Fred Parker had just prepared, crushed eggshell and all. Fred began to dole it out in tin cups. Not everyone would drink Fred's coffee; Vera claimed that coffee made the complexion muddy; she drank only tea, and that only from a glass, and only inside the hotel. Everyone else was glad enough to have a cup of Fred's fierce brew, to keep their hands warm if nothing else.

Emily continued her pep talk. "Mr. Weiss can't be with us for a while, you all know why, but as soon as his difficulties are straightened out he'll be back at the helm. In the meantime I'm in charge; come to me with any questions." They smiled and nodded without noticeable enthusiasm. Answering to a woman was not normal for them, but they would somehow make do as long as they were paid.

"Fay Winningly can't be with us, either. Miss Winningly has left the company to pursue other interests."

Emily thought she heard Mary Grace Canavan mutter, "Grand." Apart from that there was no reaction.

"Let's get to work." And they did. Emily passed out copies of the new shooting schedule. Mr. Johnson read it over, set up his camera by the stable wall, and marked off the area where the first scene was to be filmed with the usual piece of rope. The actors took their copies and squinted at them with greater or lesser degrees of comprehension. Emily was on the point of congratulating herself on how smoothly things were going without the flamboyant and controlling presence of Adam. But then Mr. Chalmers began to act up.

Emily's shooting schedule called first for a scene of Erno sorrowing over the body of Fay (to be played by Mary Grace under a blanket), next for a scene of Vera reacting with terrible grief to the news of her sister's death, and third for a crowd scene featuring a fistfight between Erno and Mr. Chalmers. Mr. Chalmers glanced at the scenario, curled his lip, sat himself down on the steps of the hotel, and reached for his flask.

Fred and Billy rushed over and began to wheedle for acting lessons. "Get lost, boys," he said to them. "The game is up. What you cannot as you would achieve, you must perforce accomplish as you may." Nobody knew what he meant by that.

Emily saw all this out of the corner of her eye while she supervised the brief shot of Erno grieving over the body of his lost love. Neither of her actors was entirely suitable for this scene. Erno looked wooden, as usual, and Mary Grace under the blanket was shivering. Crouching behind Mr. Johnson and the camera, Emily was forced to bellow at them through Adam's megaphone.

"Keep still, Mary Grace! You're dead!"

"Yes, ma'am. Can I have a hot water bottle?"

"Try holding your breath. Again. Aaand . . . action."

Mary Grace was motionless, motionless, good, but still there was no expression on Erno's handsome face. "Erno, Melpomene is bankrupt!" Emily shouted. "We can't pay you." He looked up in grief and rage; Mr. Johnson's camera caught it all. "Aaand . . . cut. Good Erno. Thank you. I was just teasing."

"I don't like to be teased," Erno said.

"Only for the movie. You were wonderful, the scene was perfect. Now go and get ready for your fight with Mr. Chalmers." She glanced back at the matinee idol and noticed a steaming black puddle at his feet that had not been there a moment ago. Fred's coffee. Mr. Chalmers coolly poured the contents of his silver flask into the empty tin cup.

He would never have dared to do such a thing right out in public if Adam were here, Emily was sure of it. She looked at the Indians; they shrugged and shook their heads. Emily was forced to address the problem herself.

"Mr. Chalmers."

"Ah! Mrs. Weiss. You elegant creature."

"Mr. Chalmers, I wonder whether you've given any thought to the scene you are to play with Erno."

"None. What's there to think about? I pound the stuffing out of him. Or he pounds the stuffing out of me. No matter. The camera grinds away, and it's all a glorious treat for the unwashed immigrants in the nickelodeons next week, to be forgotten the week after. All bilge. Why do you ask?"

"You feel that your work in front of the camera is valueless."

"I do."

He expected Emily to argue with him, to fawn over him and tell him he was the world's greatest actor. This she declined to do. "I quite agree," she said.

"Do you!" He pulled himself erect, feathers ruffled, the picture of indignation.

"You are a man of enormous gifts, Mr. Chalmers. I have watched your work with Fred and Billy, and the other day with Erno. You belong not in front of the camera but behind it, as a director. A creative force. Don't you feel that this is true?"

"Well, I — I've never given it —"

"We need you to play your part in this movie, I'm sure I don't have to tell you how desperately. But we also need your skills as a director. This fight scene. You have looked

161

over the scenario I wrote last night. What do you think it requires?"

"It requires a rehearsal."

"Brilliant. A rehearsal. Mr. Chalmers, would you do me the enormous favor of rehearsing the cast in this scene? Find Erno, explain how it's supposed to go, and run through it a few times with him."

"Mrs. Weiss, I would be honored." He put the tin cup down and went forth, nearly sober, to gather the Indians and the extras together and walk them through what was really a very complex and difficult scene.

Mr. Johnson brought his apparatus back across the street and began to set up for Vera's turn as the grief-stricken bad sister.

"That went well," Emily said to him. "Don't you think so? Erno looked good."

"You think you're going to make an actor out of that boy," Mr. Johnson said.

"One way or the other, as long as I can trick him into doing what I want him to do. Of course, he's no Robert Montmorency, but on the other hand he has no temperament and he doesn't drink. Now, for the scene where Vera hears the news of her sister's death, here's what I would like. The sunlight is coming from that way. If we spread these white sheets out in front of the steps and let the light reflect upwards, it should give a nice, diffuse —"

"Mr. Weiss said he wanted the light on Miss Zinovia to be more harsh than that."

"I'm sure Mr. Weiss would agree with me, if he were here. Now, when she comes down the steps —"

"But Mr. Weiss's idea was —"

"Dear Mr. Johnson. Until Mr. Weiss is released, which we can only pray will be soon, I am in charge, and time is of the essence."

"Yes, ma'am." They set up the scene without further argument.

"Aaand . . . action," Emily called.

Vera, the outlaw's evil daughter, waited on the front porch of the hacienda, in real life the Potts Hotel. After a reasonable interval of Vera standing and staring into the distance, Fred Parker walked onto the scene, dressed as a cowboy in boots and a ten-gallon hat, affecting a slightly bowlegged gait. He spoke a few words to her and left.

Here Emily meant to intercut a dialogue title, black with white lettering, bearing the words, "Your sister was killed during the lynching, Miss Emmy." The title would be duly embellished with the curly M for Melpomene, in case anyone in the nickelodeon audience might be unaware that they were viewing a Melpomene product. Then back

163

to Vera, nibbling her pearls, suffering acutely at the news of her sister Fay's death at the hands of the vicious lynch mob. Suffering . . . suffering . . .

"Cut!" Emily moaned. "Vera, can't you suffer more visibly than that? Wring your hands! Tear your hair! Bite your knuckles! Twitch! Do anything!" Emily had found that when Vera played a scene she appeared to do nothing at all. "I want you to show enough emotion to keep an audience interested."

"Excuse me. Konstantin Sergeyevich tells us the audience is for the actor, to improve his art. The actor is not for the audience."

"What gave him a crazy idea like that?" Emily said. "We're not running a recreation camp for actors. We're trying to make a commercial product. Even in the old country they must understand that starvation is a bad thing."

"Commercial product! *Bozhe moi!*" Vera rolled her beautiful eyes. Now, that was more like it, a good broad gesture.

"Mrs. Weiss."

"What is it, Mr. Johnson?"

"I bought myself a new close-up lens for my camera. If you'll let me I think I can use Vera's method to your advantage."

"I was hoping to finish this picture by

sundown today, Mr. Johnson."

"I brought it with me this morning. Let me try it. I think you'll like what happens."

"Very well. You have fifteen minutes to get something interesting on film. Then we do the fight scene." She wandered over to the stable to watch Robert Chalmers's technique for rehearsing his actors. He told them, put your feet here, put your hands there. Look that way, not at the camera. Swing the chair at him. Now you duck. No silly tosh about method acting.

Robert Chalmers himself would not do well in a close-up. The ravages of drink and dissipation — maybe even opium! — were stamped for all to see on that once noble visage, with his bad teeth, bloodshot eyes, bags and wrinkles that no amount of makeup could conceal. On the other hand he still had all his hair, and he had the profile, and he could make as graceful a gesture as anyone could wish. So he looked good on-screen, at a respectful distance. And he could teach his techniques to others.

Even Erno drew a small amount of benefit from being rehearsed by Mr. Chalmers. Now he was a block of wood in motion, rather than a static block of wood, and his hands and feet were in all the right places.

In twenty minutes Johnson and Vera were finished with their close-up work and the filming of the fight scene began. Emily was very pleased. The Melpomene players might almost have been a troupe of professional actors.

Just as Erno threw the first awkward punch a little fellow in uniform came riding up on his bicycle; Billy Parker restrained him from crossing the rope. "Tele gram for Mrs. Weiss," the boy said. "Sign here, please. Are yous making a movie?"

"We are."

"Gosh." He watched Mr. Johnson turning the camera, gaped at the tussling men and then at Vera, remounted his bicycle, and left.

Emily opened the telegram.

CLARENCE DARROW OTHERWISE EN-GAGED STOP BACK TUESDAY STOP WATCH OUT FOR TRUST DETECTIVES STOP STRAWFIELD

Emily stared all around. There was no one in sight who looked like a Trust detective.

THIRTEEN

At the end of the second sunny day of shooting, the company had finished *Lynching at Laramie.* Emily was very pleased with it. The close-ups of Vera shimmered with emotion, and the action scenes directed by Robert Chalmers simply crackled. She thought it was a better picture than *Revenge in the Saddle,* the one Adam had directed. She kept these views to herself when she visited Adam, along with a growing number of things she thought and felt.

Adam appeared to be lower in his spirits every time Emily went to the jail to see him. He said he was happy that Melpomene's moving pictures were being made on schedule, and that Emily was getting along fine without him, but after he stopped shaving he stopped washing, and then he stopped eating. The more that Emily was able to function without him, the less he seemed to want to live. Horrified, Emily was reduced to communicating with her incarcerated husband in chipper generalities and offering him food.

"I brought you a box of butter cookies," she said. "Here."

"Lemme see those," Chief Watson said. He opened the box and took a handful.

"No file," Emily said. "No hacksaw. They're quite all right."

"Okay," Chief Watson said. "Here." He poked the box through the bars. Adam took it, opened the box, and stared as if at a box of worms.

"Tomorrow morning we start filming the comedy," Emily said. "I need your advice on what to do, Adam." She went so far as to bat her eyes, feigning helplessness.

He sighed, stared off into space for a long time, and finally said, "Break dishes."

"What?"

"Break lots and lots of dishes, Emily. Buy a few sets on the cheap and have the actors break them. We haven't time for subtlety here. Spend a day photographing the breaking of dishes; this has always been a big success at the nickelodeon, keeps them in stitches. Fill up a reel with that. Then get busy on your melodrama. Time is running out."

She kissed her hand to him. He smelled

awful. His beautiful chin was covered with curly black hair. Break dishes?

"Right, chief," she said.

Early next morning Emily set up the scene in front of a store on the sunny main street of Fort Lee and explained the scenario to Mr. Johnson and the actors. Fred's coffee was improving. If only there were donuts. But, then, donuts too were probably bad for the complexion. The cast blew on their hands and read their copies of the scenario.

"Dishes. *Bozhe moi,*" Vera said.

"What makes you say that?"

"I do not understand the emotional truth of breaking dishes."

The woman had a point. A genius she might be, but madcap comedy was not Vera's forte. Fay would be infinitely better in the part, if only she could be persuaded to forsake the blandishments of Biograph and return to Melpomene Moving Pictures.

"We'll hold off on this for an hour, then," Emily said. "Everyone take a break. Meet me here at half past nine." She went trudging back to the Potts Hotel and telephoned Fay.

"I'm in the middle of packing," Fay said. "My train leaves for California tonight. Biograph has promised to double my salary."

"Melpomene will triple it," Emily said. "Get down to the ferry and we'll see you in an hour."

"Biograph is making me the star of their next dramatic feature."

"Melpomene will make you the star of their next dramatic feature. We start shooting it tomorrow, if we can finish this comedy today."

"Who is to be the male lead?"

"Of the comedy?"

"To hell with the comedy. Of the dramatic feature."

"Who do you want the male lead to be?"

"Erno Berg."

"All right, Fay, Erno Berg is to be the male lead of the dramatic feature. You're to be the female lead. You'll play his wife. The part will expand your dramatic range. No more fifteen-year-old schoolgirls. And with full credits. We have plans to distribute this film all over the United States and Europe. Your name will be known in Paris."

"At three times my old salary."

"Yes," Emily said. Desperate times, desperate measures.

"Very well, then. I'll see you in an hour." Now, if only the others would be as happy as Emily to see Fay return to the company.

Mr. Chalmers was the first to greet the ingénue as she alighted from the trolley car. " 'What, my dear Lady Disdain! Are you yet living?' "

"If you don't make him stop talking to me I'll turn right around and go back to Biograph," Fay said to Emily.

"Now, now," Emily said. "I'm sure we can all do our duty as professionals." She handed Fay a syrupy cup of coffee to warm her up and directed a pointed look at Mr. Chalmers.

"Ah, but of what profession?" Mr. Chalmers muttered, fortunately low enough so that Fay didn't hear him. Whatever her profession of choice, Shakespearean persiflage was plainly not Fay's strong point. Nor any other sort of repartee. If Emily had to guess she would have said that was the reason why Fay preferred the inarticulate Erno Berg to the relentlessly verbal Robert Montmorency-Chalmers. That, and the fact that Erno was younger, handsomer, and free of sour alcoholic breath.

Time to get to work. "Here's what I want you all to do," Emily said. "Make up your faces. It's a comedy. Your street clothes will be fine. Mr. Chalmers, you're the shop owner. You're very pompous and stiff. Vera, you're his richest customer. Make the most of those pearls. Erno, Fay, you're an engaged couple looking for dinnerware. You have a disagreement with Mr. Chalmers over his prices. Tempers flare. We start shooting in five minutes."

They played the scene in front of a drugstore down the street from the Potts Hotel. The store had a colorful striped awning that Mr. Johnson thought would look well on screen. The dishes were arranged in front of the store window in bushel baskets. Someday, when Melpomene had a studio with arc lights, they could film interiors inside a make-believe store. Before that happened it would be necessary to finish all four of these pictures — two Westerns, a comedy, and a drama — according to the contract with Howie Kazanow.

That's why I'm doing this, Emily said to herself. She did not believe in the emotional truth of breaking dishes any more than Vera did. It was necessary to trust Adam blindly in this. And why not? He had been a very successful moving picture theater manager. He knew the audiences. As for Art with a capital A, there would be plenty of opportunity for that when they made the fourth picture.

Emily had scarcely gotten her actors into position and begun to shoot the first scene when the trolley from the ferry slip came rolling up the street. Two men got off and drifted toward the sidewalk where the movie company was working. Emily recognized the Great Dane and the bull terrier, dressed in vested suits and soft fedora hats. The left sides of their jackets swelled with identical holster-shaped bulges. These gumshoes were taking no chances on suffering the fate of Duffy.

Fay took a plate in her hand, showed it to Erno in his role of fiancé, and the two examined the back of it. Vera fingered her pearls and looked down her nose at them. Chalmers bowed unctuously, playing his role to the hilt, the Uriah Heep of dinnerware merchants. Johnson continued to crank away. He had set up his camera in the middle of the street, right out in public. Now here came the detectives.

After all the things Johnson had told her about Edison and the Trust, even after Big Ed Strawfield's warning, Emily had failed to protect Melpomene against detectives. How had this happened? She was thinking of Art. She was thinking of deadlines. She was not thinking of ordinary security. Heaven help them now.

The Great Dane approached Mr. Johnson, scratched his chin, and pointed at the camera. Mr. Johnson shook his head at him.

The bull terrier hopped over the rope Mr. Johnson had stretched around the scene and stepped right into the frame, nearly tripping over the new M for Melpomene that the clever Fred had whittled out of wood with his big knife. Chief Watson had the old one, keeping it for evidence. Nobody wanted to use it anyway. It was all stained.

"Cut!" Emily said. "Sir, we're trying to make a moving picture here. Will you please step outside the rope?"

"Sure. As soon as I have what I came for. Are you in charge here? I thought you were a maid."

"I'm in charge here."

"Then you're the one who has Seamus Duffy's book. I've come to ask you to hand it over."

"I have no idea what you're talking about."

"If you've got it, sister, we'll find it," he said. "There's no point trying to keep it from us. We're Pinkerton men, and we get what we want."

How she longed for Big Ed Strawfield and his muscular friends. Wasn't it Tuesday? He was supposed to be back by now. "Please go someplace else to get what you want," she said. "I don't have it. And I really must insist that you take yourself out of the frame of our moving picture."

Fred got up from the porch steps of the hotel, where he had been busy whittling an extra M for Melpomene, in case another was needed.

The detective stood his ground, still spoiling the shot. "Who says you don't have it?"

"The lady says she doesn't have it," Fred said. "She asked you nicely to leave." The sun gleamed on the blade of his whittling knife. Suddenly Billy Parker had a knife in his hand too, cleaning his fingernails. Mr. Johnson came out from behind his camera. All the men, even Mr. Potts with his walking stick, began to approach the two detectives, drawn by a manly interest in potential violence.

"Here comes the eastbound trolley," Robert Chalmers said. "Why don't you get aboard it, friend? You and your colleague will just have time to catch the ferry back to New York."

"Yes, why don't you?" Fred said. "You should do that." All of the men took a step closer. Would the detectives reach for their weapons? Would they blast Emily's cameraman and all her actors to kingdom come?

The bull terrier merely curled his lip at her, ugly enough to do murder. "You haven't heard the last of us, missy."

"Oh, come on, Grogan," the Great Dane

said. "Don't be an ass. There's plenty of time. We can take care of this later." He took his companion by the sleeve and pulled him to the other side of the rope. With the whole company glaring at them the pair boarded the trolley again and left.

Ugly enough to do murder. What if these men somehow killed Duffy? Something in Duffy' memoirs, or at least in Duffy's knowledge, was so damaging to the Pinkertons that they had set a law firm and two Pinkerton operatives on him to keep it dark.

"What now, Mrs. Weiss?" Johnson said.

"What? Oh. Carry on. Do as you were doing before. Fay, Erno, you find fault with the dish. Mr. Chalmers, you become indignant. Roll film. Aaand . . . action."

Fay and Mr. Chalmers managed to work up a certain amount of dramatic tension in the scene before Fay heaved the first dish. Even Vera, though she might not have believed in its emotional truth, was able to register horror as the crockery went flying past her head. The normally wooden Erno got carried away at last, flinging the cups with gusto. Emily had to shout at him, "Erno, not at the window, the budget won't cover it, I'll have to take it out of your pay." He smashed them on the street.

When the scene reached its height, with

the dishes and their fragments flying in all directions, Emily reflected that the next scene, the very last scene of the comedy, called for Erno and Fay to run up and heave a whole set of dishes over the side of the Palisades, a gesture that Adam was certain the audience would find uproariously funny. The idea of running toward a cliff, of directing anyone else to run toward a cliff, or of running anywhere other than away from the cliff, made Emily sick to her stomach. On the other hand here was Robert Chalmers, still sober and with an excellent head for heights.

"Aaand . . . cut. Mr. Chalmers," she said. "How would you like to direct the rest of this picture?"

Three hours later, outfitted with a megaphone and a folding chair borrowed from the hotel, Mr. Chalmers was urging his dear friends once more unto the breach while Emily sat on the porch of the Potts Hotel sipping a glass of nasty, bitter Fernet-Branca and contemplating the possible suspects in the death of Duffy.

The whoops, the shrieks, the crash of crockery, all drifted over the field like something from a dream. "Now take her in your arms, Erno!" Mr. Chalmers shouted through the megaphone. "Dance! Do a crazy polka!" Emily looked up to see the pair whirling across the field toward her, laughing like idiots.

"Aaand — cut! *La commedia è finita!*" Mr. Chalmers declaimed.

Erno frowned. "What did he say?"

"He says the comedy is fine," Fay said. They danced off into the hotel, still holding each other.

Oh, spare us, not the linen closet again. "Be back here promptly tomorrow, everybody," Emily called. "We'll start filming the drama in the morning. We have seven days to complete it. Let's hope the sun shines."

Vera shook her head, fixing Emily with her tragic eyes. "The comedy is finished," she said. "Finished."

"Yes, it's finished," Emily said. "But I think it's fine, too, don't you? Audiences will love it."

"*La commedia è finita.* The phrase is in Italian," Vera said. "It means 'finished.' "

"Ah," Emily said. "Not from Shakespeare, then?"

"No. *I Pagliacci.* You are not familiar with opera?"

"Oh, yes. That's right, it's the last line of the opera, isn't it, right after —"

"After clown murders his wife and her

lover. Do you not find it odd about Fay and Erno?"

"You know how it is, Vera. Show folks."

"Erno is not show folks. He thinks Fay is virgin."

"How is this possible?"

"Erno is very young."

"But the episode in the linen closet with Mr. Chalmers," Emily said. "So loud. So public."

"Erno thinks it is misunderstanding of some sort. This is what he tells Edward."

"Okay, well, that's sort of sweet, I guess."

"She told him he was very first man in her life."

"Did she."

"And there is Mr. Chalmers, eating himself up inside with heartbreak." Mr. Chalmers was attempting to fold up his canvas chair, which resisted his efforts. He glanced up at the hotel steps and then away again with an elaborate expression of unconcern.

"Mr. Chalmers is a chaser of women from away back, Vera. If one of his quarry gets away, out of the hundreds, I can't imagine that it would bother him. You know how he is. We would hear about it if he were upset. He would be quoting Shakespeare."

"You think so? I cannot understand such light attitude in a lover. As for me, I will be true to my Edward unto death," Vera said, and rolled her eyes heavenward.

"I'm sure he appreciates that, Vera."

Chalmers at last succeeded in folding the chair. He picked it up, together with the directorial megaphone, and made straight for the hotel. Softly he murmured, " 'O thou weed, who art so lovely fair and smell'st so sweet that the sense aches at thee.' " Emily and Vera stared at each other. *Othello,* wasn't it? Another show that ended badly for the woman. Vera's plucked eyebrows went up. Chalmers climbed the porch steps, still muttering to himself, " 'Would thou had'st ne'er been born.' "

"I hope he won't make trouble," Emily said.

Vera shrugged. "Is drunken ham," she said. "I am sorry to leave you with no other acting instructor."

"Leave me?"

"I must go away."

"Surely not."

"Can you pay me for the work I have done? I must go soon."

"Are you telling me you can't be in the next picture, Vera?"

"Not possibly. I am so sorry to disappoint. It's Edward, you see."

"Actually, I don't see, but I suppose if you

must —" She dug in her purse for Vera's pay. It would be too bad not to have her in the dramatic feature, now that Emily and Mr. Johnson had finally worked out how to film her to the best advantage. But the dramatic feature was not yet written, truth to tell. In any case Emily had promised the leading role to Fay. When she sat down that night to write it, by the light of the vanity lamp, she would simply not put in a part for Vera at all. Easily done. If only she had a plot to work with. "Good luck, then." She handed the Russian actress the money and shook her little cold hand.

Mr. Potts appeared in the doorway of the cloakroom as Emily was packing up the costumes. Oh, dear, the bar bill. "What do I owe you for the Fernet-Branca?" she asked. "Mrs. Potts was quite right; it settled my stomach wonderfully." In fact she was a little tiddly.

"Think nothing of it, Mrs. Weiss; we'll add it to the bill later. I have a package for you. Could this be what you were looking for? It's addressed to your husband. My stable hand says he found it out in the weeds the other day."

Even streaked with mud, the handwriting on the bulging manila envelope was unmistakably Duffy's. Emily opened it. At last. The missing memoirs.

Just enough of twilight filtered through the dirty window of the eastbound ferry for Emily to make out Seamus Duffy's typewriting. The detective had never changed his ribbon during all the time it took him to pour out his shriveled little soul, and so the words grew fainter and fainter the more the light failed. When first she began to read, Emily was sitting all alone on a bench in the half-light in the stern of the ferry; when it grew so dark she could no longer make out the text, she looked up to find that she was no longer alone on the deck of the boat.

Fourteen

"I was born in Skibbereen, County Cork, Ireland, in 1861," Duffy wrote. "When after a long illness my father died of consumption, my sainted mother brought me together with my four sisters to America, where we settled in New York City. She took in washing to feed us. It was a terrible hard life."

"Well, of course it was," Emily murmured. "Everyone's was a terrible hard life." She flipped the pages, skimming over the education of young Seamus in the school of hard knocks. The typewriting was still clear, making it easy to skip what she didn't care about. She was looking for a mention of the Pinkerton agency, something that might offend them, something that might even prompt them to have him killed.

Halfway through the manuscript the name of Big Ed Strawfield leapt off the page at her. She flipped back to the beginning of the chapter.

THE BITTER WASH RIOT

My assignment in Bitter Wash was to worm my way into the confidence of the union ringleaders. All I had to do was take their names, my boss said, and the Pinkertons would deal with them as they deserved. Now, understand that this union was none other than the Western Federation of Miners, the scum of the labor movement. The worst that could happen to them was no more than they deserved. The WFM was the same union whose leaders, at a national meeting in 1897, told the rank and file to arm themselves with the latest model rifles and hold weekly drills so they could be strong enough to force their will on the rightful owners of the mines.

By the time I got to Bitter Wash I had been a card-carrying member of the Western Federation of Miners for five years, working undercover. It was my job for the Pinkerton agency to drift from one mine to another, ingratiate myself with the union leadership, and subvert the union in as many ways as I could.

My duties were easy, as Pinkerton

work went. It wasn't my job to put the workers and their wives and babies out of the company housing. It wasn't my job to beat up the union organizers. All I had to do was drink with them, maybe work my way up to being local union treasurer and divert their money to where it wouldn't do them any good, and get them to break the law. My boss at Pinkerton took half of what I stole and I got to keep the rest. It was a nice arrangement. When the men went night riding to dynamite the stamp mills or lynch the scabs it was the local sheriff and his men who rounded them up, sometimes with deputized Pinkerton men, but it was never me.

I came to Bitter Wash just after they called the famous strike. I made friends with some of the striking silver miners and took to drinking in the saloons with them. At first they thought I might be some kind of company man, but I lulled their suspicions by flashing my union card, calling J. J. Bohnert and the other silver bosses bad names, and talking like a socialist. All the time I was collecting the names of their leaders.

Big Ed Strawfield, the treasurer of the national union, was the worst of the lot, an ugly and violent man. A dirty murderer, too, as time would show, in spite of what a pusillanimous Idaho jury decided about it. Big Ed was nowhere in evidence in the early days of the Bitter Wash strike, being off at some other mine making trouble, but I knew him from before, and I knew the sort of man he was.

So I finished collecting the names and I gave them to my supervisor at the Pinkerton agency, McParland in the Denver office. About that time J. J. Bohnert sent to New York City for seven hundred workers to replace the striking miners of Bitter Wash, so that he could open the mines again. They hired them right off the boat at Ellis Island and put them on the immigrant train headed west. All that was left for Bohnert to do after that was to get the strikers out of Bitter Wash to make room for the new men, the scabs. The Pinkerton boss sent me back there to find out exactly where their leaders lived.

"Do you want me to put a mark over their doorways, then?" I says to him.

"Whatever will get the job done," he says.

"And what would that be?"

186

"Never you mind." And never I minded. These men were scarcely fit to live in any case, nor were their wives and children, bred up as they were to be nothing but savage anarchists and a danger to the country.

It was Big Ed Strawfield who brought the rumor to town of the seven hundred scabs coming. He rolled in on the same train as me, got off the passenger car and stood on the station platform in the blazing sun sweating and speechifying. The longer he talked the more the men came out to cheer him, until the saloons themselves were empty. I saw it was no time to be drinking with the strikers and winkling their home addresses out of them, not with the mood they were in. They meant murder and destruction, right then, that minute, of the company headquarters, the company men, and all the Pinkertons guarding the mine. Strawfield fanned the flames with his mighty rhetoric, the hot breath of his socialist lungs.

I slipped out of it and made straight for the Pinkerton stronghold, a tower they built to overlook the mine entrance and protect the scabs when they would get to town. The other Pinkertons let me in. I told them what was coming, and they gave me a gun.

It wasn't long before the strikers came, roaring for social justice. I knew Oskar Heikkinen for one of their foremost leaders, a firebrand. When the striking workers rushed the tower he was leading them. His wife and young son were with him, they tell me. Just the same I shot him dead.

The union men returned fire. Few of them were armed, and we Pinkertons had a Gatling gun to keep them out of the office and away from the mine. When the smoke cleared thirty-four of their number lay on the ground, fourteen dead, twenty more wounded, Big Ed Strawfield along with the others, I saw to that myself. Two of the Pinkertons were killed as well. By the grace of God I escaped from that without a scratch. As for the murder by dynamite of Frank Steunenberg, the murder that so closely resembled an act of the Western Federation of Miners, I'll have more to say about that . . .

The type was so faint, and the night so dark, that Emily could scarcely make out the last words on the page.

. . . further on.

But this was wonderful! What a story. Emily closed the notebook and slipped it into her bag. The waters of the Hudson slapped against the side of the boat. The ferry whistle gave a loud hoot. The engines reversed with a grind and a roar, and the boat drifted gently toward its berth at the 128th Street ferry slip.

Emily looked up to find the Great Dane regarding her gravely. She gasped in alarm, and covered the gasp with a fake coughing fit. Never show fear.

"Interesting reading, Mrs. Weiss?"

"You have the advantage of me. I don't believe we've been introduced."

"Holbert Bruns is my name. I'm with the Pinkerton National Detective Agency, as you probably remember."

"Mrs. Adam Weiss. Melpomene Moving Picture Studios." She gave the huge man her hand. He pressed it gently and released it. He could have crushed it to a jelly if he wanted to. If he wanted to, he could have crushed her entire being to a jelly. She was terrified. There was nobody else in this corner of the ferry. The other passengers were getting off. In her mind she searched herself for useful weapons. How badly could she disable this man with a hat pin? She wished she had Duffy's gun with her, but she had left it behind in the Knickerbocker, hidden in the pocket of Adam's good overcoat.

"I want to apologize for the behavior of my colleague, Mr. Grogan, this morning," Mr. Bruns said. "He's new on the job. I'm supposed to be training him."

"Ah. Well, if you'll excuse me, Mr. Bruns, I believe the ferry is docking. I really must be going."

"Allow me to accompany you."

"No, that won't be necessary, Mr. Bruns, I'm perfectly —"

"I want to explain my problem to you."

"I have my own problems, Mr. Bruns. Now, if you'll please just —"

"Mr. Seamus Duffy's manuscript, which you have in your bag there, is a tissue of lies."

"All I have in my bag is a movie scenario."

"Mrs. Weiss. I can see that you're an intelligent woman. Respect my intelligence, please. Don't try to play games with me. Mr. Duffy wrote a pack of lies calculated to discredit the Pinkerton National Detective Agency, an institution that for the past fifty years has been all that stands between law-abiding Americans and the bloodiest kind of anarchy. I must ask you to give it to me."

"Have you read it?"

"No."

"Then how do you know it's a tissue of lies?"

"Just give it to me. I'm sure you don't want any trouble."

"As I told your ill-mannered colleague this morning, Mr. Bruns, I haven't got it."

"Then what was that you were reading just now?"

"A scenario."

"What's a scenario?"

"A plan for shooting a moving picture. A list of scenes, what goes on in them. A story for a movie."

"Why don't you let me see it? Then I can judge for myself."

She put her hand into her bag, closed her fingers around a notebook, pulled it out, and handed it to him.

"There's not enough light to see it," he said.

"No, there isn't. Why don't you simply take my word?"

"I have a better idea," he said. "I'll just take this back to the office where I can read it in a good light."

"Oh, I wish you wouldn't."

He chuckled, a deep rumbling sound. "I'll

191

bet you do. But never fear, Mrs. Weiss. If it's as you say, I'll give it right back to you tomorrow. I promise you I'm a man of my word." He tucked the notebook under his arm and joined the stream of passengers leaving the ferry.

Vera, loitering by the gangway, had seen them talking.

"Who was that?" she said.

"The Pinkerton fella who came looking for Mr. Duffy's memoirs this morning," Emily said.

"So he wouldn't believe you didn't have them."

"I do have them. Lend me your shawl for a few minutes."

"You are cold?"

"I am scared." She wrapped herself up in cashmere and black fringe until she looked like a Middle Easterner straight from Ellis Island. "Any minute now that man is going to get a good look at the notebook I gave him, and see that it's not Duffy's memoirs."

Vera raised her eyebrows, but she said nothing. The Great Dane loped away eastward in the direction of the elevated, not stopping under any of Mr. Edison's many streetlights to take a look at the notebook under his arm. He would have had to open it to see what it was, anyway. Nothing was written on the outside of Emily's film notebook. On the inside, there was only . . . oh. Her address at the Knickerbocker Hotel. An intelligent woman, the man said. Yes, aren't I?

At the end of the ferry ramp Big Ed Strawfield was waiting for Vera. She flew into his arms. They kissed for a long time. Emily waited, the black cashmere shawl folded over her arm. Vera whispered something in Big Ed's ear. He turned to look at Emily.

"So you have Duffy's memoirs," he said.

She gave the shawl back to Vera. "I have to get back to the hotel and develop this film," she said. "The comedy went very well, I thought. Wait 'til you see Vera in it. She was quite funny, even in a small part. Quite the comedienne. It's always good to increase one's range, don't you think?"

"You should come with me, now, Mrs. Weiss," Big Ed said. "We have things to talk about."

"Vera is leaving the company. I was sorry when she told me that."

"Vera is very loyal to me. She thinks you should come with me, too, don't you, pump-kin?"

"Come along, Mrs. Weiss," Vera said. "We go to my apartment. I give you some tea. Is important we talk."

"I have so much to do. Can't this wait 'til tomorrow?"

"You have Duffy's memoirs," Big Ed said. "And I'm reasonably sure you read them." He grabbed her by the arm and encouraged her down the street toward the subway station.

"Watch the film can," she said. "Don't make me drop it. A whole reel of *Silly Sally* is in there and it's precious stuff."

"Vera, give her a hand with her bundles. And take her other arm. Make sure she comes with us. I must have a long talk with this lady."

"Wait! I can't keep up with you, you're walking too fast!"

"Konstantin Sergeyevich teaches us that one must walk by beginning the step with the heel, so, and rolling forward on the foot. You are walking like the dancer Isadora Duncan, stepping first on your toes. Here, Mrs. Weiss. I show you how to walk. Swing your legs from the hips. Have you done your exercises? You must see that your knees work like springs. Step off from the tip of your great toe, so. Good."

And then they were in the subway station, where the guard waited to take their tickets. He should be told she was being kidnapped.

Or somebody should. If only these people would let go of her arms she could reach her hat pin. Then they would see who had the upper hand. Of course if she stabbed Big Ed with that paltry five-inch hat pin it would scarcely slow him down, a man who could survive bullet wounds. She would have to strike like a snake and then run like the wind, pushing off from the very ends of her big toes and flying through the air like a stork. Even more unlikely, she would have to leave the precious can of film behind. "Let me have the film, would you please, Vera? I would feel so much more comfortable if I held it in my arms. All that work."

"I think not," Big Ed said. "I think we'll keep control of the film until we get to the apartment, don't you, Vera? That way Mrs. Weiss won't try to run off. Here's the ticket chopper. If you say anything to the guard I'll open this film can and expose it to the light."

The guard, a little weasely man, took the three tickets that Big Ed held out to him and dropped them into the chopper. Emily said nothing. The man didn't look as though he'd be much use in a scrap anyhow, even if *Silly Sally* and a whole day's shooting weren't at risk.

The train roared up to the platform. With

her springy new walk Emily was able to keep up well enough to prevent her arms from being torn from their sockets as they carried her along into the last car, which was otherwise empty of passengers, and sat her down between themselves on the long bench. For several stops the three sat shoulder to shoulder, staring into space, swaying with the motion of the train, not speaking.

Emily was thinking about what she had read in Duffy's memoirs. "He shot you, didn't he?" she said finally, shouting to be heard over the noise of the train. "Duffy shot you during the Bitter Wash riot."

"Somebody did, I guess," he said. "Was it Duffy? Doesn't matter, the wound is all healed up."

"You owed him an ill turn so you waited your chance and murdered him."

He laughed. "Aren't you afraid to be down here in the subway train with me? Such a terrible man might throw you onto the tracks."

"I'm not afraid of murderers," she said. "I'm afraid of heights."

FIFTEEN

There were no heights between the subway station where Ed Strawfield dragged Emily off the train and the third floor walk-up in Greenwich Village some three blocks away where he and Vera lived, and so Emily was able to keep from succumbing to panic. On the way to the apartment she saw a beat cop and some friendly looking passersby she could have called out to. *Help! I'm being kidnapped!* It crossed her mind a couple of times to do this, or to try in some other way to escape from Big Ed's clutches. But they still had the precious can of film. Besides, what she had said to him was true; she felt no real fear of him. What she felt was curiosity. She knew that Seamus Duffy's version of the Bitter Wash riot was only half of it, maybe even less than that. She wanted to hear the other side of the story.

The apartment would have made a wonderful movie set. All it needed was arc lights.

Deep purple velvet draperies separated the front room from the back and hung across the windows; throws and pillows covered with barbaric embroidery lay swooning on the damask chairs; a huge samovar surrounded by glasses dominated a highly polished table. The décor could not have been more Russian.

"Would you like some tea?" Vera said.

"Yes, please." Emily assumed it would not be poisoned. She sat down in an embroidered armchair.

"Tea!" Strawfield said. "Vera, the lady is starving to death and so am I." He took a seat in the chair next to Emily's. "Make us some sandwiches, will you?"

"With pleasure," Vera said, glaring at him. She moved the curtain aside to pass into the back part of the house and revealed a number of half-packed traveling bags. Frilly underwear drooped out of a suitcase onto the oriental rug.

Emily's stomach rumbled. A sandwich would be nice. She looked up to find Big Ed Strawfield skewering her with the gaze of his single eye.

"So you want to talk to me," she said.

"Yes, I do. You're an intelligent woman, a fair-minded woman."

"People keep telling me so."

"I want to explain how things were in Bitter Wash. I can imagine what Seamus Duffy had to say. I want you to hear what I have to say."

"Go ahead, then. Explain the Bitter Wash riot to me."

"First of all I don't want you to call it the Bitter Wash riot. Only the bosses and capitalists call it the Bitter Wash riot."

"What do you want me to call it, then?"

"Call it what it really was. Call it the Bitter Wash massacre. Sixteen people died in that fracas, and some of them were women and children."

Vera appeared with a tray, black with hand-painted flowers, very Russian, laden with salami sandwiches on pumpernickel and beer. No tea. She placed it on a table before them.

"And so Duffy shot you," Emily said. The sandwiches were very good.

Strawfield was not shy about talking with his mouth full. "Duffy shot me, yes, but he also shot and killed Oskar Heikkinen. A better man than Oskar never lived. He shot Oskar Heikkinen's son, who was just a child."

Vera perched on the arm of Strawfield's chair and began to nibble a sandwich. Emily wondered whether Konstantin Stanislavsky had taught her to sit like that.

"Do you understand what I'm saying? Seamus Duffy shot a child. Imagine what Mrs. Heikkinen must have felt, her husband dead in her arms, her young son bleeding. And all those other widows. Duffy and the Pinkerton guards slaughtered the workers where they stood, without mercy. Have you ever seen a Gatling gun? You crank it like a movie camera, and it spits death, over and over. You can't call Bitter Wash anything except a massacre."

"How did it start, though?"

"From the beginning? You mean at the end of the Civil War, the long slide of the currency into deflation? The bombing of the Haymarket Square rally in Chicago? The panic of '93? Or maybe the election of McKinley, a miserable tool of the eastern banking interests, who chose to ruin the farmers and workers by keeping the country on the gold standard?"

"What was the proximate cause, I guess you'd call it. Tell me what happened in Bitter Wash."

"Okay. In Bitter Wash, there was a silver mine, owned by one J. J. Bohnert. There was a push to put the currency on a silver basis, and so the owners were looking forward to a tremendous rise in the price of silver. But things changed. McKinley got elected on a hard currency platform, and the price of silver went down."

"Quite a bit, as I recall."

"Yes. Mine owners all over the west increased the working hours for the miners from eight to ten hours a day and cut per ton scale by ten percent. Eleven-year-old boys were working ten hours a day in those mines. The accident rate was horrendous. Another worker was killed every three or four days."

"Per ton scale. What's that?"

"The money they pay the miners for every ton of ore they dig. The miners in J. J. Bohnert's mine in Bitter Wash went out on strike in the heat of the day. Do you know what it's like out there in Bitter Wash?"

"Mr. Strawfield, I'm a Down East Yankee. I've never been west of Rumford Falls."

"This'll give you an idea," he said. He produced a photograph from somewhere. "It's like the backside of hell."

Very like. The main street was a ribbon of dry, blowing sand with an old dog limping across it; the dwellings were mean, flat shacks in need of paint; a pile of tailings rose up in the background, half a mile high. You could see a water tower in the picture, and far away across the desert, some mountains. Emily had never seen anything so desolate and dry.

"The miners were living in rented company housing, buying their food and supplies from the company store. Do you think the rent went down ten percent? Or the price of food? Do you think their families were ten percent less hungry?"

"So they went out on strike," Emily said.

"Yes."

"And the bosses — J. J. Bohnert — hired the Pinkertons to come and break the strike."

"The Pinkertons and seven hundred scabs, poor ignorant foreign cattle. Naturally they had to make a place for these men to live before they arrived in Bitter Wash, so J. J. Bohnert had his lapdog, the sheriff, deputize the Pinkertons and throw the striking miners out of their houses. When I got to town they were living in tents in the desert."

"That desert?" Emily said, looking at the picture. She was unable to imagine a more inhospitable landscape.

"The very place. So I came to town and said a few words, and we marched peacefully on the company headquarters to present our case to J. J. Bohnert. You know the rest."

"Duffy shot you."

"To tell you the truth I didn't recognize him when I first saw him on the ferry slip, with a bald head and no mustache. Only later, in the wig —"

"Show her your scars, *lyubov,* where that horrible little man shot you," Vera said.

"Would you like to see my scars, Mrs. Weiss?"

"No, thank you, your word is good enough for me, Mr. Strawfield."

"I'm glad to hear it. After the massacre was all over Boss Bohnert called Governor Steunenberg, who sent the state militia to mop up the strikers and make sure the scabs got safely to the mine."

"Mop up how?" Emily said.

"In the night the militia and the Pinkerton men raided the workers' tents. The rank and file with their wives and children were loaded into boxcars, shipped out of state, and dumped off in another desert on the other side of the mountains. The leaders of the strikers were fingered by Seamus Duffy to be arrested, tried, and hanged. It was the end of the Western Federation of Miners in Bitter Wash."

"What did you do?"

He lifted his chin. "I lived to organize another day, in other mines. I'm in the

Industrial Workers of the World now, and my life is dedicated to justice. We're through fooling around. I want to see the revolution." His eye flashed. It was a sight to put on a labor poster.

"But if they were hanging all the leaders in Bitter Wash, how did you escape?"

"Oskar Heikkinen's widow hid me from the Pinkertons until I was well enough to travel. A very generous woman. She was taking care of her son, you see, so nobody noticed that there were two gunshot victims in her tent instead of one." Big Ed drank off the last of his beer and banged the glass down on the table.

"And what of Duffy?"

"Duffy made a lot of enemies. He wasn't just a spy, you know. He was what they call a provocateur."

"What did he provoke?"

"Violence. He burrowed into the confidence of union men all over the West and talked them into committing rash acts. There are people who say he gave the dynamite to Harry Orchard to blow up the governor, just so they could pin it on me and the Western Federation of Miners. See if he talked about that in his memoirs. I'm betting he didn't. There'd be a rope waiting for him in Boise if he admitted to that."

"So you're saying the miners wouldn't have done any dynamiting without . . . without provocation."

"Without provocation, no dynamiting." His eye glinted.

"There must be many people who would have liked to see Seamus Duffy dead."

"Wherever there are workingmen you'll find enemies of Duffy and the Pinkertons."

"I see," Emily said. "Now that I know the whole story, I guess I'll be going. Thank you for the sandwich."

"I want to say one more thing, Mrs. Weiss. Seamus Duffy was an insignificant little man, a mere instrument of the ruling classes, a stooge and a dupe. Bigger villains than Duffy were pulling his strings."

"Then you really didn't hate him enough to —"

"Having said that, I must add that Duffy deserved to be killed as richly as any man who ever drew breath. You didn't see the look on his face when he was firing into that crowd of miners, some of them no older than twelve."

"My husband is in jail for killing him, Mr. Strawfield. He may go to the electric chair. You know he didn't do it."

"I know he didn't do it, you're right."

"I thought you were dedicating your life

to justice."

Big Ed scratched his head, gnawed his lip, rubbed his bad eye. "I tell you what, Mrs. Weiss. I'll see what I can do for your husband."

"Clarence Darrow won't help him."

"Something other than getting Clarence Darrow to defend him." He put his huge hand on her hand. "I promise."

"Thank you."

"Vera, do we have any pie?"

"We have cake," she said. "Would you like cake?" But Emily wasn't thinking about food anymore. She was thinking about Big Ed Strawfield getting off a train, making a speech, leading a crowd of downtrodden miners against a powerful silver baron and his Pinkerton henchmen.

"It strikes me that your story would make a great movie," she said. "Will you help me write the scenario?"

"If you call it the Bitter Wash massacre. It wasn't a riot."

"How about *Massacre at Bitter Wash?*"

Sixteen

In the morning the sky over Manhattan was black with rain clouds. No one was traveling to Fort Lee on the ferry except for a truck driver, a few charwomen, and a small crowd of colorful people on their way to some studio where the producers had enough capital to film under arc lights. Melpomene Moving Picture Studios would be able to do that, too, on some not far distant day. Emily carried the completed scenario for *Massacre at Bitter Wash* in her bag, coauthored by Big Ed Strawfield, and it was a ripsnorter. Bold, honest, riveting, dramatic, it was bound to make Melpomene a million dollars.

Emily saw a woman she suspected of being an actress inside at the refreshment stand, buying the ferry line's offering of stale peanuts. She carried a huge puffy handbag, probably a makeup case with space left over for costumes. Surely an actress.

"A rainy day for making movies," Emily remarked.

"Actophone has a studio in Coytesville," the girl said proudly. "We work indoors with lights."

Act-o-phone, Emily thought, or Ack-*toff*-inny? When she got to the jail she would ask Adam with his classical education whether the girl got it right. "Nice for you. Independent company?"

The girl turned pale. "Don't tell anybody I mentioned the studio. Forget you heard anything about it. You're not a detective, are you? I thought they were all men."

"They probably are all men. But you're right; you want to be careful what you say to strangers." She put out her hand. "I'm Emily Weiss. I'm an independent producer. Melpomene Moving Picture Studios."

Her smile was lovely. "I'm an actress. You can call me Gwendolyn Gwynne. Really it's Leola Dietz."

"Are you under contract?"

"I am, but only until the end of this picture."

"Give us a call when you're free, Miss Gwynne. Adam and Emily Weiss, at the Knickerbocker Hotel. Or at the Potts Hotel in Fort Lee, when the weather is good. We might have something for you." We might still be doing business as Melpomene Moving Picture Studios, in spite of everything. We might even have our own indoor studio with a whole battery of whacking great arc lights and make movies twenty-four hours a day.

With warm feelings of optimism Emily strode into the Fort Lee police station and shook out her umbrella. A splendid future awaited her and Adam in the moving picture business. In spite of Mr. Edison's best efforts, independent studios were popping up right and left. Fantastic movie plots dropped from the sky. Actresses came in on every ferry. She could hardly wait to get her teeth into *Massacre at Bitter Wash.* Before Melpomene Moving Picture Studios could prosper, of course, a few tiresome details had to be settled, such as getting Adam out of jail.

"Morning, Miz Weiss." Chief Watson mumbled his words around a large plug of tobacco. "You're looking cheerful this morning."

"Why not? I have every confidence that your judge is back from Florida, and I'm here to post bail for my husband."

"No. Sorry." He opened the lid to the

potbellied stove and spit in it.

"I'd like to visit him, then."

The chief replaced the stove lid askew, leaving it partly open, and reached for his ring of keys. "Got any more interesting pieces of evidence for me? Like that wallet you mysteriously produced?"

"No. Sorry."

"I only ask because a lady about your size and shape robbed Mr. Duffy's boarding-house yesterday."

"That's shocking, Chief Watson. It's a good thing the police in Fort Lee are better at preventing such crimes than the police in Manhattan."

His little pig eyes narrowed. "How did you know Mr. Duffy lived in Manhattan?"

"I looked in his wallet."

"Thought you might have done that. *Ptooie.*" The lump of chaw sailed through the air and fell in the stove with a disgusting sizzle. "Come on, then."

Like a man attending a nickelodeon show, the chief pulled up a chair to watch their meeting. Once again Emily was prevented from giving Adam a true picture of her recent activities.

"Morning, darling," she said. She directed a peck at his cheek through the bars. He still hadn't shaved. He looked like a vagrant.

His breakfast dish rested on the concrete floor in front of his cell door, sticky with uneaten oatmeal porridge, buzzing with flies.

"Morning, Emily. Six days, and God knows when this rain will end." Still the voice of impending doom. She took a deep breath, determined to stay cheerful. Who was it that signed that insane contract, anyway? Not her. "I delivered the second and third movie to the processor this morning," she said.

"Good, sweetheart. Good. How's the final movie coming? The drama?"

"I have a great story for it."

"You made it up?"

"Someone told it to me. It's history. Something that happened a few years ago. Here." She handed him the scenario she had worked out with Big Ed Strawfield, complete with mustard stains and salami grease on the pages.

"Dramatic, is it?" Adam said.

"Very dramatic. Did you ever hear of the Bitter Wash massacre?"

"The Bitter Wash riot. Sure. A classic union-management conflict." He thumbed through the pages, squinting at certain scenes. "You must have been talking to Big Ed Strawfield."

"And other sources," she said, glancing at Chief Watson. He was cleaning under his nails, his attention flagging. Probably he would be as delighted to have Duffy's memoir as any of the Pinkerton men, and she would give it to him, if she thought it would do Adam any good, and if she didn't need it for color in the *Massacre at Bitter Wash* scenario. When she got back to the hotel she planned to finish reading it. Perhaps it would contain that crucial piece of information that the Pinkertons would kill to suppress. Then all she would have to do was figure out how they got to him, in the middle of a crowd of actors and extras, with the whole thing being filmed.

"So what's your story?" Adam said.

"Everyone seems to agree that the immediate cause of the confrontation was the speech Big Ed Strawfield made to the miners after he got off the train in Bitter Wash."

"Sounds good," Adam said. "The train comes into town. Good cinema, a big steam train, bearing down on the audience. Make 'em gasp."

"I wonder where we can get footage of a steam train on such short notice," Emily said. "The movie has to be finished by next week."

Chief Watson's head came up. "Go to

Hackensack."

"I beg your pardon," Emily said.

"Hackensack. Trains come through all the time. You can get there from here on the trolley."

"Oh. Thank you, Chief. All right, perhaps we can — it's too overcast today for filming actors, but a large black steam engine ought to show up nicely against a cloudy —"

"Telephone Mr. Johnson," Adam said. "See if he's free this afternoon."

Chief Watson chuckled. "So you're going to make a movie about Reds," he said. "Wobblies."

"And why shouldn't we?" Emily said. "It's still a free country."

"You and your husband oughta be in jail. But, that's right, he is in jail. Haw, haw."

"Anyway the movie isn't about Wobblies," Adam said, closing the notebook, raising his magnificent (if hairy) chin, his unfocused eyes seeing something grand. "It isn't about politics at all. It's about a beautiful young mother in mortal peril."

"It is?" Emily said.

"Yes!" The light began to come back into Adam's eyes for the first time since the death of Duffy. "Heikkinen — the first miner who was shot, right? He had a young son."

"Right," she said. "I didn't realize you were familiar with the story."

"We'll change all the names, anyway. Heikkinen, or whatever we call him, will be played by Erno Berg. God knows he looks Finnish enough." Adam was actually smiling.

"He is Finnish, is why. All right, Erno plays Heikkinen," Emily said. She took out a small notebook and made an entry.

"We'll make Heikkinen's son an infant. A helpless babe in arms. The beautiful wife will be played by Vera Zinovia, with her dark, haunted eyes."

"Vera quit the company yesterday," Emily said. "She and Big Ed are going back to Russia."

"Okay, then, sweetheart. The beautiful wife will be played by Fay, with her long golden hair. Innocence personified. You can roll up a bath towel from the hotel for the baby, if you can't find a convincing doll on short notice."

"Fay . . . plays . . . a grown-up," Emily murmured, writing it down. "That's good, Adam, I told her she ought to do that."

"It's high time, don't you think?"

"Higher than you can possibly imagine," Emily said. "Yes, yes, you're right, darling. I think she's ready."

"There's a mob scene, though, when the massacre takes place. What about that? Can we get more extras?"

"I have spare footage from *Lynching at Laramie* for the mob scene," Emily said.

"Good girl. Now, write this down."

"Right, chief."

"J. J. Bohnert — that will be Chalmers — has lustful designs on Heikkinen's pretty young wife, which is why the miners went out on strike in the first place."

That couldn't be right. "An interesting view of the roots of class struggle," Emily said.

"I'm the one who's been to college, sweetheart. I studied history. Don't talk to me about class struggle. To continue. As soon as Heikkinen is shot, which happens as a result of Bohnert's evil manipulation of the miners' union, Bohnert goes after Fay. She no longer has a husband to protect her. With the helpless baby in her arms, she rushes out into the desert, her curls streaming in the wind. Just south of Fort Lee there's an empty field you can use for the desert."

"We're not going to have her put her hair up, then."

"No. The girlish look works better here. Now she stumbles, her little feet ensnared in a sudden patch of quicksand. She

215

clutches the helpless infant to her breast and raises her delicate hand in supplication to the Almighty. J. J. Bohnert comes after her, drawing ever closer." Crouching on tiptoe, Adam spread his hands out and crept up on the bars of his cell. "Now he stands over her, with an evil leer." Emily held her breath.

"Then what happens?" Chief Watson said.

"See the movie," Adam told him. "Got it, Emily? Your audience is hooked. That's the way you want to write it." He handed her notebook back to her.

"We need someone to play Big Ed Strawfield."

"Why not Strawfield himself?"

"If he's still in town. Okay, I'll try him."

"And don't forget to go to Hackensack today for that train footage."

"Yeah. Hackensack," the chief said. "That's where you want to go today." Smiling, he started back to his office.

"May I use your telephone?" Emily asked him.

"No. I need it myself." He closed the office door.

"Thanks. I'll just find my own way out," Emily said. The Potts Hotel had a telephone she could use.

■ ■ ■ ■

The operator told her the number she had for Vera and Ed was no longer in service. Emily called the candy store where Mr. Johnson could be reached; after a short while he came to the telephone; she asked if he could come with her to Hackensack and take some pictures of a speeding locomotive. "While we're at it we can have Fred and Billy dress up as miners and wave at the train. Let me give them a call at their boardinghouse and get them to meet us here at the Potts Hotel. The trolley from Fort Lee goes straight to Hackensack."

"Good," Mr. Johnson said. "I'll see you shortly."

Two hours later the sun had come out from behind the clouds and a small crew from Melpomene was clustering on the platform of the station in Hackensack, where the twelve fifty-eight was expected momentarily. A freight train approached out of the west, roaring and swaying. The boards trembled under Emily's feet. The train did not stop, nor yet slow down, but flew right through the station, tearing at Emily's hat, pulling at her face, sucking the breath from her lungs.

Mr. Johnson cranked his camera, recording for all time the power of the mighty steam engine before it barreled onward to the city with its cargo of apples, iron, coal, and hoboes. The dust settled. The footage would look wonderfully Western.

All at once Emily had an unpleasant feeling of rabbits frolicking on her grave. She was seeing Chief Francis X. Watson rushing to his telephone after advising her to go to Hackensack. Who had Watson been telephoning? It could have been a Trust detective, or even Edison himself. F.W. could be Francis Watson.

"Mr. Johnson, it might be that a Trust detective will show up here looking for us," she said.

"Think so, do you?"

"I do. If one does come, it means that Chief Watson has betrayed us."

"Wouldn't surprise me."

"We'll keep our eyes open," she said. "Billy, Fred, be ready to flee at a moment's notice. We may have some company from the Trust."

Five more minutes passed without a train coming through. A few people came and stood on the platform. The sun came out. With a jingle of harness a horse-drawn bread wagon approached and parked by the side of the station. Emily studied the writing on the wagon, then the advertising signs posted here and there on the walls and the steps of the station: BUTTERNUT BREAD, BABBITT CLEANSER, LUCKY STRIKE CIGARETTES, J. D. GREEN, UNDERTAKER. Mr. Johnson shifted the position of his camera until he was looking down the track with the station on the right side of the frame.

The bread man got out of his truck and watched them. "You making a movie?"

"Yes, we are," Emily said.

He was fascinated. "The wife and I go to the movies all the time. Are you with Biograph? We like Biograph movies the best."

"No, we're Melpomene," Emily said. "A new company. We're better than Biograph. Would you like to be in our movie?"

"Very much. What do I have to do?"

"Go and stand with the boys over there. Do what they do."

"This is wonderful! Just wait 'til I tell the wife."

A bell rang. The passenger train was coming.

And here it came, charging down on them at first and then slowing, brakes squealing, bell clanging, steam hissing out from somewhere between the wheels. It coasted past Mr. Johnson until the hindmost door of the hindmost passenger car came level with his camera.

Emily raised her megaphone. "Now, Billy and Fred, and you, Mister Bread Man, get between that door and the camera!" she shouted. "We don't want to see Eastern passengers on a Western railroad train. Wave! Cheer! Big Ed is on this train. He's coming to save your jobs and frustrate the aims of the evil bosses. That's it! Keep it up!"

Though there were three passenger cars, only a handful of passengers disembarked from each of them at one o'clock on a weekday afternoon. When they realized Mr. Johnson was making a film they all began to grin and wave, all except one burly man stepping grimly off the very first car behind the tender.

Mr. Johnson continued to crank away. Billy and Fred in their miner costumes and the bread man in his uniform effectively blocked the camera's view of grinners and wavers, even the wag flapping both hands and calling out, "Look at me, Ma! I'm in a movie!" The steam was helpful, too, swirling around the engine until the big red S on the side (for New York, Susquehanna and Western) was all but hidden. Melpomene could always pretend it stood for Santa Fe, but most moviegoers would know they were looking at an Eastern train.

The man at the front of the train, neither grinning nor waving, froze at the sight of Mr. Johnson and the camera. Had to be the Trust detective, with that cheap-suit quality about him that Emily had learned to recognize. "Aaand . . . cut! Let's get out of here," she said.

"Right. I see him," Mr. Johnson said. "It's McCoy." He folded his tripod with all speed.

SEVENTEEN

A sudden cloud of steam roiled out from under the passenger train. Emily could no longer see the man Johnson said was the dreaded McCoy. "Bo-oard!" the conductor sang out. With a shudder and chug the train began to move.

"Hide!" Emily said.

Mr. Johnson stared all around. "Where can we hide?"

"In here," the bread man offered, opening up the back door of his wagon.

In the wagon was a long stick with a grabber on the end, for reaching for high bread loaves. "Can we borrow this?" Emily said. "And a loaf of bread?"

"Er —"

"And this piece of canvas." Emily clipped the loaf of bread onto the end of the grabber, threw the canvas over the whole thing, and handed it to Fred. "Go," she said. "Hold this as if you were carrying a camera and tripod, and you and Billy make that man follow you. Can you do that?"

Fred laughed. "We'll string him along all the way to Coytesville." He slung the rig over his shoulder, making believe it was heavier than it was. It looked very much like a movie camera. "He won't bother you again."

"If he catches us he'll be sorry," Billy said.

"Splendid. But, remember, don't kill him."

"Here he comes," Billy said. "You hide now."

Before the steam had cleared Emily and Mr. Johnson were snugly ensconced in the back of the bread wagon, with the real camera and tripod tucked down under a stack of fresh warm cinnamon buns.

"Looks like you were right," Johnson muttered. "Chief Watson set us up."

"I wonder what else Chief Watson is guilty of," Emily whispered. "You know, he was right there when Duffy was killed." Johnson grunted.

The bread man climbed into his seat in the front of the wagon and slid open the little window between them. "You owe that feller money?"

"Sshh," Emily said. "He's a Trust detective, trying to wreck our movie. Don't give us away. I'll pay you a hundred dollars to drive us to Fort Lee."

"What about my bread route?"

"What about five hundred? Plus five dollars for your part in the movie, of course."

"For five hundred you can have the horse, the wagon, and all the bread."

"It's a deal," Emily said, opening her purse, not as bottomless as it had seemed last week. Desperate times, desperate measures, once again. Perhaps they would find a use for the bread truck. But could she or Mr. Johnson drive a horse? "Will you drive us to Fort Lee?" she said to the bread man, handing him the money. "You can come back on the trolley. I'll even give you carfare."

"Won't be necessary. Glad to do it. I don't s'pose you need me to be an actor anymore."

"We can always use actors. Can I have a cinnamon bun?" By the growling of her stomach Emily realized she had missed her lunch again.

"Lady, they're all yours now."

"Would you like one?"

"No, thanks."

She ripped open the waxed paper package and waved a cinnamon bun at Mr. Johnson, who was peeking out the back. "Bun, Mr. Johnson?"

"Beg pardon? Oh, no, thanks." He opened the door a hair wider. "Look at that. He's going after Fred and Billy, all right. But they're too fast for him. They'll lead him all the way to perdition."

"Hope he doesn't stumble across the Actophone studio," Emily said.

"The who?" the bread man said.

"Actophone. Ac*toff*inny. Another independent film company. They have a studio in Coytesville, someone told me."

"Oh, well, that ain't our worry," Mr. Johnson said.

The bread man said, "Giddyup."

Back in Manhattan later that afternoon Emily called Vera's apartment again. This time the operator told her that the telephone had been disconnected. Gone. She needed to know more about the Bitter Wash story. It was true that Adam was going to work his magic of poetic license. Still it would be good to check the real facts before they started filming. If while fact-checking she happened to shed any light on Duffy's murder, so much the better.

The New York Times was practically next door to the hotel, and Emily nearly went there to do her research, until it occurred to her that the *Times* was too stuffy to publish pictures. Nothing brought a story to life for her like a visual representation of the participants. But the *Times* was only one newspaper out of many in New York. A few blocks away were the offices of the *New York Journal,* a paper whose accounts of Bitter Wash were sure to be illuminating in all the right ways.

The switchboard operator-receptionist who presided over the front counter of the *Journal* sent Emily up to the third floor. As she stepped out of the elevator the pungent odor of printer's ink and stale tobacco struck her in the face. "The morgue is in the back," the elevator boy said. He pointed the way through a sea of desks, almost all of them occupied by men in shirtsleeves smoking cigarettes. Some were typing, some talking on the telephone, some shouting, "Copy!" and some staring off into space, or staring at Emily as she passed. Beyond them a chest-high oak counter loomed, festooned with newspapers threaded onto wooden rods and presided over by a young man wearing a green eyeshade, maroon arm garters, and ink-stained white celluloid sleeve protectors. The smell of printer's ink grew more intense as she approached the counter.

"Excuse me. Is this the morgue?"

"We prefer to call it the library. How can I help you?"

"I'd like to see some old stories. Anything you have on the Bitter Wash massacre."

"Ah, yes. The riot. Just a moment," he said. He went into the files and emerged moments later with a long, narrow manila envelope, open on the short side, with "Labor: Violence" typed on the protruding flap. It was full of clippings, all marked in blue pencil "Labor: Violence," and stamped in red ink with various dates. She poured them out on the counter.

"Take as long as you like," the young man said, "but don't take away any of the clips, and don't mark on them. Try to keep them in order. If you need your own copy of anything, make a note of the date and we'll sell you a back issue of the paper." He gave her paper and pencil.

"Thank you," she said. As the clerk resumed his previous activities Emily began to unfold and study the fragile clippings.

BOHNERT MINE REPLACEMENT WORKERS KILLED IN BOXCAR EXPLOSIONS

WESTERN FEDERATION OF MINERS BLAMED; BIG ED STRAWFIELD SOUGHT

Three hundred out of seven hundred replacement workers (Strawfield would call them scabs) had been killed outright in the explosions, most of the others wounded. Some had their families with them. Dead women, maimed children. Big Ed Strawfield was certainly a determined man.

The story of the Bitter Wash riot was lightly covered, being only one incident in a long string of clashes between capital and labor in the West. Many involved the Western Federation of Miners, a violent group that demanded outrageous privileges for the workingman, ruinous to the interests of company shareholders, for example, an eight-hour workday.

Here was another story that mentioned Edward Strawfield:

FRANK STEUNENBERG SLAIN IN EXPLO-
SION
DYNAMITE WIRED TO GARDEN GATE
WESTERN FEDERATION OF MINERS SUS-
PECTED

Dynamite again. Alas for Governor Steunenberg, the man who sent the state militia to round up the union ringleaders to be hanged, the man who transported the rank-and-file union members and their families in boxcars to a pitiless desert. He came home to his house in Caldwell, Idaho, one evening, all unsuspecting, opened his garden gate, and was blown to kingdom come. Lawmen found a hanger-on of the Western Federation of Miners in a nearby saloon with fuses and wires in his pockets. Under questioning the man implicated Big Ed Strawfield.

The case came to trial. So this was the real trial of the century. Nothing to do with the beautiful Evelyn Nesbit on her red velvet swing. Many stories appeared in the *Journal* during the course of the trial.

As Emily read them, all in chronological order, things looked bad for Big Ed. Harry Orchard, the hanger-on who had rigged the explosives, swore under oath that Big Ed and the Western Federation of Miners put him up to it. But defense counsel Clarence Darrow said no, the dynamite and the plan for the murder came from one of Orchard's associates, an alleged Pinkerton provocateur traveling under the name of Jack Simpkins. No one knew what had become of Simpkins. He had done his work and kept right on traveling. If indeed he ever existed.

Seamus Duffy was nowhere mentioned in the account. Emily wondered whether Duffy had anything to say about the trial in his memoirs. She had hidden the manuscript in the hotel room under a pillow in the bottom of the chest of drawers, planning to finish reading it as soon as she had the time.

Clarence Darrow's rhetoric was considered to be one of the great national treasures of the twentieth century, good enough to sell newspapers, and so the *Journal* had run his entire summation. It covered several pages, which had been folded to fit in the clip envelope and flattened with a round pencil, the way the clerks at their desks behind the counter were doing with today's clips. Each clerk worked on top of a stack of papers in a hypnotic rhythm: bang a long strip of brass on the stack, tear off a column along its edge, fold up the clip, and rub it with a pencil. Clunk, rip, fold, rub.

Emily shook herself and returned her attention to Darrow's summation. He praised the nobility of Big Ed and the patience of Big Ed's aged mother, who was sitting in the front row, until there could hardly have been a dry eye in the courtroom. He extolled the dignity of labor, and denounced the rich. Evidently no one on the jury was rich. About the man who actually did the murder, he said: "I don't believe that this man was ever really in the employ of anybody. I don't believe he ever had any allegiance to the Mine Owners' Association, to the Pinkertons, to the Western Federation of Miners, to his family, to his kindred, to his God, or to anything human or divine. I don't believe he bears any relation to anything that a mysterious and inscrutable Providence has ever created. He was a soldier of fortune, ready to pick up a penny or a dollar or any other sum in any way that was easy, to serve the mine owners, to serve the Western Federation, to serve the devil if he got his price, and his price was cheap."

Stirring stuff, but not a word of it sounded to Emily like logical proof of Big Ed Strawfield's innocence. As far as she could see, Mr. Darrow had dazzled the jury with flaming, empty oratory. She tried to imagine him defending Adam. What would he say? Something empty and stirring, moving the jury to turn him loose without knowing why.

She gave the clippings back to the library clerk and bought a couple of back issues of the paper, one with a brief summary of the trial and one with a story about the Bitter Wash riot, as they called it. The riot issue showed engraved sketches of the principals. The leader of the rioters was a Finnish miner who vaguely resembled Erno. Duffy wore a mustache then, and had more hair; he looked almost the same as he did the day he was killed. How she longed for a good night's sleep. She folded the papers under her arm and headed for the Knicker-bocker.

EIGHTEEN

The sun was down by the time Emily left the offices of the *New York Journal,* the streets of the city ablaze with electric lights. Still traveling by foot rather than by subway, she walked in the front door, straight past the pompous doorman and the loafing bellboys, instead of coming in by the Times Square Station entrance on the lower floor as she usually did. When she passed the desk, the clerk waved her over and said that someone had left a package for her.

"A package!"

"An envelope, rather. Here it is, Mrs. Weiss." He handed her a sealed nine-by-twelve manila envelope with metal prongs. She tore it open.

A note was in it, dated the day before, scrawled in a hasty and spidery hand:

Dear Mrs. Weiss,
  Edward and I must go home to Russia

now as a result of the cruel oppressions of your government. Edward asks for you to give this note together with Duffy's manuscript to police chief in Fort Lee to make him let Mr. Weiss out of jail.

Edward says he's sorry for any trouble he may have caused you.

Warmest regards,
Vera

What note? She felt in the envelope. Ah, here it was:

To Whom It May Concern:

I wish to confess to the murder of Seamus Duffy, dirty scabloving agent of capitalist oppression and former Pinkerton detective. When I saw him on the set of Mr. and Mrs. Weiss's movie I remembered everything he did in Idaho and Montana against the workingman. I became enraged and stabbed him through the heart with the nearest sharp object, which was the iron stake to which the Melpomene trademark was fastened.

I can't really say I'm sorry. The world will be a better place without him.

Sincerely,
Edward Strawfield

Apparently Big Ed Strawfield never expected to return from Russia to face prosecution for the murder of Duffy. He was gone for good. The authorities must have been after him for some other crime. Wicked as he was, though, Big Ed had done the decent thing and given Emily the evidence to gain Adam's release. What a man! Even though he was a cold-blooded killer. Emily must take this letter to Chief Watson at once, together with Duffy's memoirs. The memoirs explained everything. The confession wasn't anywhere near convincing without them.

Later on she could get something to eat. Maybe she could even have a late supper with Adam, if she could get him out tonight. Hold him in her arms without the odious Chief Watson standing over them. She took the elevator straight up to her room to get the memoirs.

Jimmy, the elevator boy, said Mr. Weiss's brother from Boston was waiting inside.

"What brother?"

"He said it was supposed to be a surprise." The elevator cage slid open with a clang. Down the hall she could see yellow light spilling out of the door to her room.

"I don't remember Mr. Weiss's brother," she said. "What does he look like, would you say?"

"Little short man, shorter than me," the boy said. "Clean shaven. Dark hair. Wiry."

"Rather like a bull terrier in appearance?"

"Now that you mention it."

"Bad news, Jimmy. Mr. Weiss is an only child," she said. "Go back down to the lobby and send up the house detective." She stepped off the elevator.

"Don't you want to wait for the house detective, ma'am?"

"It might be too late," she said. "Hurry."

Quietly, quietly she pushed the door to her hotel room open. Even with his back turned to her Emily had no trouble recognizing Grogan the Pinkerton man pawing through her underwear and cursing softly to himself. The mattress was thrown half off the bed, the covers in disarray. All Adam's clothes were scattered from hell to breakfast.

He hadn't touched the bathroom yet, but he wouldn't have to, would he? Duffy's manuscript was in the bottom drawer, right there by Grogan's knees.

He slid the drawer open.

Emily put her hand to her hat and plucked out the hat pin. Five inches of cold steel. Or maybe it was warm steel by now; she had been indoors for a while. Maybe it wasn't even steel; maybe it was tin, or some similarly ineffectual substance. She had never

236

actually used a hat pin for a weapon. The Pinkerton man reached into the bottom drawer and pulled out Duffy's manuscript with a grunt of satisfaction.

Emily crept up behind him and stuck the hat pin about a sixteenth of an inch into his neck.

"Ow! What the —"

"Don't move," she said. "Drop it."

He stayed on his hunkers, very still, for a count of about three. Then he sprang free of the hat pin, brought his fist around, and punched her in the face. Emily went flying backward through the air. She hit the door to the room and slid down it like a rag doll. Stars twinkled and popped everywhere.

"Lady, I don't know why you want this so bad, but you're not keeping it," Grogan said. "I told you before; we Pinkertons get what we want." He kicked her smartly in the ribs. "Out of my way. Come on, move."

She found enough strength somehow to slide back up the door. The coat tree was within reach. She took hold of it to steady herself.

Obviously a hat pin was not a useful weapon for making threats. Emily supposed she could have killed the man outright if she had stuck it in his neck all the way, instead of trying to scare him with it, but —

! No, for making threats you need brawn, or a firearm. Like Duffy's gun, for instance, here in the pocket of Adam's good overcoat. She closed her hand around it.

"You Pinkertons get what you ask for," she said, "and, boy, are you asking for this." She shot him in the instep of his left foot. The revolver recoiled violently with a deafening roar.

He dropped the manuscript. "Jesus *Christ,* lady!"

"I'm sorry. Did I hurt you?"

"Shit! Shit! Shit!"

Evidently so. He rolled around on the floor, biting his lip and uttering more curses, while Emily gathered up Duffy's memoirs. A few pages had fallen out. Fortunately they were numbered. As she slipped the last loose page back in the binder the house detective arrived, accompanied by the elevator boy, his eyes like dinner plates.

"I heard a shot," the house detective said.

"I had to shoot him. He attacked me," Emily said.

"Your *ass,* lady! Listen, I'm a Pinkerton agent engaged in the performance of his duties! This woman — ow — Christ —"

"Go get the doctor, will you, Jimmy? Good boy. Now then. What are you doing in this lady's room?"

238

"That manuscript is not her property!"

"What manuscript?"

"I don't know what he's talking about, sir," Emily said. "As you can see, he attacked me." She pulled her hair back and showed him her eye.

"You're going to have quite a shiner there, Mrs. Weiss."

"And he kicked me in the ribs."

"In the performance of my duty! Look! Here are my credentials!" He pulled the wallet out of his coat pocket and flipped it open.

"Pinkerton man. Armed, too, I see. I'll just take that," the house detective said, lifting Grogan's gun from its shoulder holster. "Well, Mr. Pinkerton man, I don't care who you are, or what you think you're after. You're not allowed to beat up defenseless young women in the Knickerbocker Hotel."

"Defenseless! Ow! Ow!"

It must hurt to get shot, Emily reflected. She wondered whether Big Ed Strawfield had carried on like that when Duffy shot him.

"And your gun, too, please, ma'am, if you don't mind."

"Oh. Certainly." She handed it to him. He twirled the cylinder and took out all the bullets.

239

"I'll put this in the hotel safe for you, Mrs. Weiss. You won't be needing it in the Knickerbocker. I'm in charge of your personal safety. *He* won't give you no more trouble, that's for sure." He dragged the wounded man to his feet. "Keep your door locked, ma'am. I'll have them send some raw steak up to you from the kitchen; see you put it on that eye."

After the door was closed and bolted behind the men the first thing Emily did was to have a look at the can of film. It was intact and sound. The next thing was to bathe her face in cold water, hoping to stop the room from going around. It helped a little bit. Taking a deep breath was painful, but maybe that was only bruising.

She thought about trying to get the confession and Duffy's manuscript to the police chief in Fort Lee before the last ferry: staggering out in the dark, stumbling around Manhattan dizzy as a coot, with pains in her chest every time she breathed in, encountering the second Pinkerton man who would surely be lying in wait for her. Maybe others of his kind as well. The Pinkerton agency feared Duffy's book. They would stop at nothing to get it. No. Better to stay right here. Too bad for Adam, but he must spend another night in the pokey.

To atone for leaving her poor Adam in jail she got busy and made title cards, pausing only to go to the door when she heard someone knocking.

"What is it?" she said.

"Room service," answered a very deep voice. "I've brought you your steak."

"Stick it under the door."

"It won't fit under the door."

"Then take it back downstairs and cook it."

"The house detective says you need it for your eye."

"Well, I don't. Take a walk, Mr. Bruns. Leave the hallway. If you're still there by the time I count to ten I'll give you what I gave your confederate."

"Listen, Mrs. Weiss, I only want to talk to you. I'm sorry about Mr. Grogan's behavior. I told you he was a new man. Actually he was on probation. The Pinkerton National Detective Agency has let him go. He no longer works for us."

"One —"

"I'm prepared to offer you a great deal of money for Seamus Duffy's memoirs, Mrs. Weiss. What would you say to an offer of five hundred dollars? I'm sure that's more than you could gain by publishing it."

"Two —"

"My job is on the line, here, too, Mrs. Weiss. I have three children to support, and another one on the way. If I don't bring my boss those memoirs by tomorrow I'll lose my position. We'll all be put out in the street. We'll starve. Sweet little kids. Would you like to see pictures?" A small sepia-tone portrait came sliding partway under the door. She could just see two little boys in starched clothes with big collars, sitting stiffly in some photographer's studio. Maybe they were Bruns's children.

"Three —"

"Mrs. Weiss, you don't want me for an enemy. I can be very unpleasant. Anytime, anywhere, you might run into me. I can be behind you in the subway when the train is coming."

"Four —"

"I can come into your room at night, when you're asleep. I can get next to you in the middle of the Hudson on the ferry, or on the top of a cliff in the Palisades. Give me the manuscript. Take the money."

"Five —"

"Oh, hell." His footsteps receded down the hall.

Her hands were shaking like crazy when she went back to her work.

NINETEEN

The next day dawned cold and misty, with a sharp smell of smoke that grew sharper as the early ferry chugged across the Hudson. When Emily came in out of the chill to secure two dressing rooms for the day in the Potts Hotel she found Mary Grace Canavan mopping the floor.

"Morning, Mrs. Weiss."

"Good morning, Mary Grace."

"Here early, ain't you? Jesus, Mary, and Joseph, look at your eye."

"I've come to get Mr. Weiss out of jail before the movie company arrives."

"How you gonna do that?"

"He's innocent."

"Is he more innocent than he was yesterday?"

"He's always been completely innocent. But now there's proof."

"Oh."

"I have here a confession signed by Mr.

Edward Strawfield. He killed Mr. Duffy."

"No, he didn't." Mary Grace wrung out the mop, dripping with gray water.

"Yes, he did, he says so right here," Emily said.

"He's lying, then. I was watching him the whole time we were shooting the movie."

"You were?"

"Mrs. Weiss, you told me to watch Big Ed Strawfield. I watched him. I seen him when he didn't do it."

"How can this be?"

"It just is. It is, Mrs. Weiss. But you go ahead and get your husband out of jail. I won't say nothing to nobody."

Me neither, Emily assured herself. Nothing to nobody. Getting Adam out of jail was the main concern now. Then he could take charge of making this last movie, and she could try to find out who . . . a sudden image of the dead body of Duffy flashed into her mind, M for Melpomene protruding from his chest. Okay, so Big Ed didn't do it. Maybe Big Ed's enemies did it, the Pinkerton men. Maybe they somehow infiltrated the crowd of extras, unseen by the movie company, unfilmed by the camera. Maybe it was the mysterious Simpkins. But why would Big Ed then confess to the deed?

Or maybe it was Chief Watson himself.

Duffy keft that graft notebook in a file with Watson's name on it. Clearly Watson was being blackmailed; he was standing right next to Duffy when he was killed. . . .

No time to worry now about that now. Emily must spring Adam from Watson's grip and get the filming of the last movie under way. "Is Mr. Potts awake yet?" she asked Mary Grace. "I want to rent two dressing rooms again today."

"He ain't back yet from the fire."

"What fire?"

"The fire up to Coytesville. One of them movie studios burned down. He's a volunteer, you know. A huge fire it was. All the fire companies turned out."

"Good heavens."

"Mrs. Potts is there, too, making coffee for the firemen. It was quite a show. I ran up there in my nightgown to take a look. Somebody said detectives from the Trust set it on fire. What's the Trust?"

"Enemies of the independent moviemakers," Emily said. "But surely they wouldn't resort to arson."

"Well, that's what they're saying. Are you and Mr. Weiss in dependent moviemakers?"

"Yes."

"Better watch out, then."

■ ■ ■ ■

Chief Francis X. Watson arrived to open up at seven thirty that morning, after Emily had been sitting on the front step of the Fort Lee police station for a good twenty minutes, perusing Duffy's memoirs. Beneath Duffy's anti-union vitriol a very interesting story was unfolding. Duffy, Steve Adams, and Harry Orchard had just arrived in Caldwell, Idaho, with a suitcase full of dynamite and begun to inquire after the residence of former governor Steunenberg. What would happen next? Could it be that Duffy himself was the elusive Jack Simpkins? She glanced up from under the feathers of her hat and saw the chief standing there jingling his keys in his hand. The chief's face and hands were black with soot and his clothes reeked of smoke.

"Good morning, Mrs. Weiss."

"Good morning, Chief Watson."

"I've had quite a night, little lady, quite a night."

"Is the fire out?"

"It's finally out."

"They're saying it was arson, that a Trust detective burned the studio down."

Chief Watson frowned. "I wouldn't know

anything about that."

She tucked the memoir back into the manila envelope and followed him into his office. "I have something for you. This is a confession signed by Mr. Edward Strawfield. He sent it to me when he left the country. And this is the memoir that Seamus Duffy wrote before he died. It explains why Mr. Strawfield might have wanted to kill him. I've put a bookmark in the page where Mr. Duffy talks about Bitter Wash, Idaho, what went on there, what the Pinkertons did."

Chief Watson levered the potbellied stove open. "Freezing in here," he said. Yesterday's *New York Journal* lay on the floor next to his chair; he crumpled it up and mashed it into the stove.

"As you can see," she said, "my husband is innocent. This is the proof of it. Now you can let him go."

"Hmm," he said. "That's as may be." He put a few sticks of kindling on top of the newspaper, followed by a chunk of hardwood, set a match to the paper, and rubbed his dirty hands together over the fire before he replaced the lid.

"Here," she said. "Read these."

Watson pulled out a pair of gold-rimmed glasses and hooked the earpieces over his ears. Squinting, he examined the confession note. "Huh," he said, and began to flip through the manuscript.

"You want to read the part where I placed the bookmark," she said. Or maybe not. Maybe the chief was searching for some mention of his own name, some reference to how Duffy was blackmailing him, something about the Big Mitt Ledger.

"Have you had a chance to read all this, Mrs. Weiss?"

"No," she said, looking straight at him. "I read only the part that would help my husband."

He seemed startled at the sight of her face, and she remembered her purple eye. He shrugged and looked at the note again. "I wish someone could tell me why a man who fought tooth and nail to beat a charge of murder in Idaho would confess to a killing in Jersey."

"It's beyond me, Chief Watson," Emily said. "Still, there it is."

"Looks like your husband is innocent, all right."

"He is," she said. "He is innocent." She thought, You knew all along he was innocent, you distressing clown, because you did the murder yourself. Oh, if only there were some trustworthy law enforcement official she could deal with. The evidence to convict the chief was probably in the memoirs she had just handed him.

As if he were having the same thought the chief tightened his grip on the manila envelope. "I'll let your husband out right now," he said. "First let me lock these papers in the evidence drawer."

Mrs. Potts had returned from the Actophone studio fire by the time a battered Emily and a bedraggled Adam showed up at the hotel needing breakfast. She laid out a feed of bacon, eggs, toast, coffee, and cider, even though, having been up all night long, she was not in much better shape than they were.

"Would you like some more toast, darling?" Emily said. "I'm afraid you've lost weight. That jacket is just hanging on you."

"It's wrinkled," Adam said. "That's the only trouble with it. I had to roll it up and use it for a pillow. No, thank you, no more toast. Actually I feel wonderful, sweetheart. For the first time in a week — imagine, that jackass kept me locked up for a week! — I feel like a human being. The nobility of hardship is a lot of romantic bushwah. My shoes won't stay on! The jackass claims to have misplaced the laces. He threw them in the stove, that's what I think."

"Why would he do that?"

"He pretended to believe I was going to use them to hang myself."

"Listen, Adam, a lot of things happened while you were inside, things I couldn't tell you about because Chief Watson was standing there."

"Complete jackass. I tell you, Emily, if I had known when I started out last week what I was going to be forced to endure I would have worn my buttoned shoes." He ran his fingers through his hair. "Now I need a haircut."

"Darling, it had to be Chief Watson himself who killed Duffy. It was either him or one of the Pinkerton men. It definitely wasn't Big Ed Strawfield."

Adam laughed. "Are you sure the culprit wasn't little Fay? Don't be silly, darling. The man confessed. I wonder if there's a good barber in Fort Lee. Where did Mrs. Potts go? I'd like another cup of coffee."

Emily raised her arm to summon Mrs. Potts and grimaced.

"Something wrong?"

"A pain in my ribs. I think it's only a bruise." Emily's eye was throbbing also, and swollen almost shut. It must be turning wonderful colors. Even Adam noticed.

"You didn't finish telling me about your eye, sweetheart."

"There's nothing much to tell. I went back to our rooms and found one of the Pinkerton detectives rummaging through our things. When I tried to make him stop, he —"

"How many days before the contract is up? Is it five, now, or four? You know, if this weather holds, four days will be plenty of time to shoot this picture. You told the actors to be here this morning early, didn't you? I want to start right in on shooting."

"Yes, they —"

"Howie Kazanow came to see me in the jailhouse, can you believe it? To gloat over my misfortunes, I suppose. I told him to go and — but, you know old Howie. Insulting him is just like pouring water on a duck."

"Actually I don't know Howie, Adam. We've never met."

"Incidentally there were some parts of your scenario that looked an awful lot like socialist propaganda to me, sweetheart. Big Ed talking, I suppose. I cut those parts out. So what do you say we call the picture *Riot at Bitter Wash?* I think that will play a lot better in Peoria than calling it *Massacre.*"

"No."

He cocked his head on one side and

looked at her oddly, as if he might have heard wrong, but then he said, "Okay. What do you think of this, then? We can have three or four scenes of the labor leader's beautiful young wife fleeing across the pitiless desert with the baby in her arms before the evil mine own er catches up to her and grabs her."

"Fay could play that part quite well, I should think."

"Right."

"And instead of a desert we can film it on the side of the cliff," Emily said. "It'll be more dramatic." It was a spiteful little gesture on Emily's part. She was disappointed to find that it didn't make her feel any better.

"Great idea," Adam said. Outside the trolley bell sounded. "Ah! The actors are here. Go and give them their copies of the scenario for the first scenes and get them started with costumes and makeup, sweetheart, while I rewrite the last few scenes."

"Right, chief."

The trolley had left by the time Emily got to the front porch to greet her actors. The wind, still smelling of wood smoke, drove a cloud of dry leaves rattling down the street. She drew in her breath at the cold and felt a sharp pain in her chest. And so she knew better than to gasp again when she saw, standing among the actors, the tall, tweedy form of Holbert Bruns.

He was watching her with a particularly unsettling look. Penetrating even. Her high school Latin teacher used to give her that look to show he knew she hadn't studied her lessons; Ricky Schwartz used to give her that look to show he knew what she looked like without any clothes. She felt the color rising in her cheeks. This wouldn't do. Ignoring him pointedly, she turned her attention to the actors.

Fay Winningly and Erno Berg were in rare high spirits; Emily had never seen Erno laugh before. Robert Chalmers had the look (and the odor) of a man who had been up all night drinking.

Fay was the first one up on the porch. "What are we doing today, Mrs. Weiss?" she said. "Oh, my God, look at your eye." Everybody looked at her eye.

"You'll all be happy to know that Mr. Weiss has been released from jail," she said. "Someone . . . someone else has confessed to killing Mr. Duffy."

"Someone confessed?" Erno said. "Who? Who confessed?"

Robert Chalmers seized her hand and

253

breathed into her face. Whatever he had spent the night drinking, the fumes were enough to fell an ox. "Does this mean I'll no longer be directing? Oh, dear lady. You should put a piece of steak on that."

"Thank you, Mr. Chalmers. I'll see to it later. Yes, Mr. Weiss will be directing from now on. Cast, Mr. Johnson, here are your copies of the scenario for the first scenes of *Massacre at Bitter Wash.* Erno, you will be Oskar Heikkinen, the noble leader of the labor union. Fay, you will be his beautiful young wife. Mr. Chalmers, you will play J. J. Bohnert, the arrogant silver baron."

Erno looked at his part with a strange dense frown, almost as if he couldn't read English. Perhaps he couldn't.

Fay said, "So Mr. Weiss is out of jail," and smirked at her. Emily thought, She believes Adam beats me, and she likes the idea. We'll just see who has the last smirk, my sweeting, when you're dangling off the cliff in act three. Seventeen years old. Emily looked long and hard at her, almost a movie stare. What else about that girl was false? Aside from her heart. Those childlike hands. Was there blood on them?

Chalmers flipped his pages. "A labor drama."

But Adam didn't want it to be a labor

drama. "Actually it's about lust and the reckless abuse of privilege," Emily said. "A classical theme, don't you agree? Biblical, even."

"Mm," Chalmers said. "Yes. Old Testament. The story of Uriah the Hittite in modern dress."

Mr. Chalmers liked it! Emily was astonished. In her secret heart she had been thinking that Adam had taken Big Ed Strawfield's clean, fine story of class struggle and perverted it to pander to the coarse taste of the movie audience. But, no; it was changed into something that mirrored the Good Book itself, a classic drama, a work of Art. Adam was surely a genius, or if not a genius, a man gifted beyond Emily's mundane powers of understanding. No wonder he had moods. Uriah the Hittite. Who the hell was he?

But time was passing. "Makeup and costumes, everybody," Emily said. "Erno, the noble plainsman outfit, Fay, the prairie housewife dress, Mr. Chalmers, the bloated capitalist getup with the stickpin. Fifteen minutes."

The actors rushed inside. Mr. Johnson came up the steps and squinted at her. "If I had an eye like that I'd get a leech put on it," he said. "Do you a lot of good. Bring down the swelling."

"Thank you. I'll keep that in mind."

"Is Mr. Weiss inside?"

"He's revising the later scenes. I believe he wants to start shooting in the stable yard, to match the mob scene footage left over from *Lynching at Laramie.*"

"Then I'll try to get the same camera angle as before. Hope this smoke clears away." The air was still thick and sharp-smelling from the Actophone fire. Mr. Johnson carried his camera away into the far end of the stable yard. Now there was no one on the street but Holbert Bruns, giving Emily the movie stare this time. Slowly he walked to the foot of the hotel steps.

"Mrs. Weiss."

For a long moment Emily thought of running away from him, of rushing inside and huddling next to Adam, a comforting presence even though he was oblivious to her needs and concerns this morning. But since when had she not fought her own battles? She stood her ground. The Pinkerton man approached, the sound of his feet loud and hollow on the wooden steps, and stood looming over her.

"Mr. Bruns," she said.

His lower lip hung down as he studied her black eye. "Did Grogan do that?"

"Yes."

He put his finger under her chin and tilted her face up, almost as if he meant to kiss her. "I don't wonder you shot him," he said. "I'd like to shoot him myself, and not in the foot. I can't tell you how sorry I am." The wool of his tweed coat had a faint sheep smell. "Have you tried putting a wet cloth on that eye?"

"Yes. It's better than it was."

"Well . . . well, I'm sorry."

She took a step backward, out of range of whatever it was he was exuding. "Thank you for your solicitude, Mr. Bruns. What brings you to Fort Lee this morning?"

"I've come to see you, Mrs. Weiss."

"Here I am."

"Yes." He looked searchingly into her face again, then frowned and drew a paper out of his inside coat pocket. "Mrs. Weiss, my employers have authorized me to offer you a thousand dollars for Mr. Duffy's memoirs and for your future silence on the matter. I have here an agreement, which, if you will sign on this line —"

"I'm afraid that's impossible. I don't have Mr. Duffy's memoirs anymore."

"Where are they, then?"

"My husband —"

"Your husband has them? Perhaps I'd better talk to him."

"My husband has been in jail for the past week, charged with the murder of Mr. Duffy. Perhaps you know something about the murder of Mr. Duffy."

"Only that he's dead."

"Perhaps you would remember more about Mr. Duffy if I called him Jack Simpkins."

Now she had his complete attention. "Where is your husband now, Mrs. Weiss? I can't tell you how important it is for him to let me have those memoirs."

But Adam was in the upstairs hall rooting through Mr. Potts's desk, trying to find a pencil. A week in jail in this town was as good as a year. Nothing stayed where he remembered leaving it. As a result he was reduced to stealing.

The door to the men's dressing room was slightly ajar. Through the crack he could hear giggles, emanating from Fay, and through the frosted glass he could see the blurred form of Erno Berg taking his shirt off.

"Don't make fun of me," Erno said.

"I'm not making fun of you, my only love. I'm making fun of your itsy-bitsy scar. It looks like a bullet wound. Come on, now, where did you get it? Did somebody's husband shoot you? Hold your eyes still, I have to darken your lashes."

"Somebody's husband? I'm not that kind of man, Fay." Adam knew he shouldn't be listening, but, what the hell, it was interesting drama. Unlike what Erno was doing on camera.

"Every man is that kind of man. You aren't very old yet, or you would know it. . . . Oh, don't look at me like that, I didn't mean it, darling. Of course you're not that kind of man. Please pretend I never said that. Make a mouth for me now, dearest, and I'll put some lipstick on you."

Here was a good number two pencil with a nice long point and an unused eraser on the end. Adam eased the desk drawer shut, turned to sneak away, and caught his sleeve on the sharp spike of Potts's bill spindle. Damn. It made a pick in the smooth twill weave. His jacket looked bad enough without being poked full of holes.

Erno was speaking very low. "Tell me something, Fay. Tell me the truth."

Presumably the concierge at the Knickerbocker could tell Adam where to find a good reweaving service. Shame to spoil a good coat.

"What?" Fay said.

"How many men have you had?"

Adam stopped to listen again. He was curious about that himself.

"Twenty, thirty, I don't know," she said.

"You're still laughing at me. I told you to stop."

"I've stopped, then. I'm not laughing."

"So tell me the truth. I wasn't the first, was I?"

"No, dear, you weren't the first."

"Did you do it with that drunken old ham?"

"Why would you think that?"

"The maid said so."

"She's crazy."

"And the cook said so."

"The cook is crazy, too. Really, Erno, this is too wearisome. Hold still while I paint your lips."

"You did, didn't you. God. You disgust me."

"Erno, sweetness, let me explain something to you. I do what I want. I'm not a little girl anymore. I'm — I'm twenty-four, far older than you, with a world of experience you can't even begin to imagine. Of course men have been a part of that."

"You slut."

"Oh, now it's 'you slut.' First it's 'Fay, come to bed with me, I adore you, I can't live another day without you,' and then, after I give you what you want, it's 'you slut.' "

"You lied to me."

"You lied to yourself, Erno. Get away from me. Do your own makeup."

"Dirty lying slut."

The conversation was becoming embarrassing, the more so if Adam got caught listening to it. He crept away and down the stairs.

TWENTY

The intensity of Holbert Bruns's complete attention was almost more than Emily could bear. "My husband doesn't have Mr. Duffy's memoirs, either, Mr. Bruns. I gave them to the chief of police here in Fort Lee so that he would let my husband out of jail. The memoirs are important evidence, you see, taken together with Mr. Strawfield's written confession."

"Strawfield's — you're not telling me Strawfield confessed to Duffy's murder!"

"You're surprised."

"I am. It seems odd."

"It makes more sense when you read Mr. Duffy's memoirs."

"And that's why you fought so hard to keep them, to clear your husband."

"Of course."

Bruns tilted his hat back and scratched his head. "I like you, Mrs. Weiss. I don't know why, exactly. I think you're a very dangerous woman."

"Surely your wife would do the same sort of thing for you."

"My wife?"

"The mother of your four children." Emily took the picture out of her bag and gave it back to him. "Or three, wasn't it, and one on the way."

"Yes. Thank you."

"Will you really lose your job over this?"

"Yes. Sylvia and I will have to go back to Oshkosh and live with her mother now." He sighed and pulled a long face. "By the way, Mrs. Weiss, I didn't mean it when I said I'd throw you under the subway."

"I didn't mean it when I said I'd shoot you," she said. "Couldn't have done it anyhow."

"Why not? You shot Grogan."

"The hotel detective took my gun away afterward."

"I must say that's something of a relief, Mrs. Weiss." He was almost good-looking when he smiled.

"And how is your Mr. Grogan?"

"Oh, he's . . . he's hobbling around. I wouldn't let *him* get close to me on a subway platform, if I were you." Bruns looked over her shoulder; someone was standing in the hotel doorway.

263

Adam had come through the door without letting it squeak. Emily took him by the hand. "Adam, dear, may I present Holbert Bruns? Mr. Bruns, this is my husband, Adam Weiss."

"Mr. Bruns," Adam said, nodding. "I like the coat, but it may be a little too Eastern. Emily, how soon will the other actors be ready? I'd like to get started as soon as possible. Here's the revised scenario for the last few scenes."

"Five minutes or so. They're getting dressed right now," Emily said, taking the papers from him.

"I'd still like to have Big Ed Strawfield in this," Adam said. "But since he's gone, we'll have to — say, Mr. Bruns, I think we can use you. You're about the right height. With a little padding —"

"Use me?"

"You're an actor, aren't you? We need someone to play Big Ed Strawfield in *Massacre at Bitter Wash.* With the right makeup and an eye patch —"

"*Massacre at Bitter Wash?* You're making a movie out of the Bitter Wash riot?"

"It's a very dramatic story, I'm sure you'll agree," Adam said.

"May I see the script?"

"We don't have another copy. Your part

would be very simple, though. You have only to stand on a soapbox and shake your fist."

"As Big Ed Strawfield. I see. Tell me, what part do the Pinkertons play in your movie?"

"None, actually," Adam said. "We didn't have enough actors to put the Pinkertons in. Do you want to take the part of a Pinkerton? I really don't think you're the type."

"No, no. I only thought — you know, they're very litigious. They'll sue you at the drop of a hat."

"The Pinkertons," Emily said.

"Yes."

"I don't think they'll raise any objections to our scenario, Mr. Bruns," Emily said. "As Mr. Weiss wrote it, it's straight out of the Holy Bible."

"Big Ed Strawfield in a Bible story," Bruns said.

"To a degree," Adam said. "Will you do it?"

"Yes. When do we start?" His broad grin made Bruns look less like a Great Dane and more like a wolf. Emily wondered whether this persistent canine quality of his would come through on film. With enough makeup, maybe not.

"In five minutes," Adam said.

Emily told him to go upstairs to the men's

dressing room and get Mr. Robert Chalmers to make him up as Big Ed Strawfield. "Tell him I sent you."

"Yes, ma'am. Big Ed Strawfield. Me! Ha ha!" He turned and rushed up the steps of the hotel, still laughing.

Adam, contrariwise, was not laughing. "Did I hear that actor say you shot someone?"

"Holbert Bruns is . . ." She was going to say not an actor, he's a Pinkerton operative, but then Adam would have had a fit and kicked him off the set, and Big Ed Strawfield would never even be mentioned in the movie. She really wanted Big Ed Strawfield in the movie. In a sense it was Strawfield's story. "He's hearing rumors," she said.

He took out a cigarette and lit it, scratching the match on the door frame. "And are the rumors true?"

"About my shooting someone?"

"Wouldn't have been Erno, would it?"

"No. Why?"

"It seems your Finnish beau has a bullet hole in him."

Good heavens. "Is he all right?"

"It's an old wound, evidently." He blew out a long stream of smoke through his nose.

"Really. How strange." Bullet holes didn't

fit with Emily's notion of Erno Berg as a model of clean Nordic manhood. "How did you find that out?"

"Never mind that. Listen to me, Emily. I want a straight answer. Have you been shooting people?"

"I put a bullet in a very disagreeable Irishman yesterday."

"My God."

"In fact I blew a hole in his foot. He was beating me up at the time."

"You really shot a man in the foot."

"I did."

"I don't know you anymore. You aren't the woman I married, that's for sure."

"If I hadn't shot him you'd still be in jail," she said. "He was stealing Duffy's memoirs."

"Emily, I don't have time for this," Adam said. "I'm telling you. Stop playing girl detective. Unless this picture is finished by sundown tomorrow we lose everything. That's all I care about right now."

"So who do you think shot Erno?"

"Stop it."

"Just tell me."

"Somebody long ago. Fay thinks it was a jealous husband."

"She would, wouldn't she."

"I don't know what you have against that

girl, Emily. She's all right. She's had some bad breaks."

"She's older than you are, Adam. Did you know that?"

"No, she's not."

"I've seen her birth certificate."

"Sweetheart, you're losing your mind." He turned to go back into the hotel, shouting, "Places in five minutes!"

Emily wandered over to where Mr. Johnson was fooling with the alcohol lamp in his camera.

"Cold out here," Mr. Johnson said.

"Certainly is," Emily said. She glanced over at the hotel and saw Adam moving around in the window of the women's dressing room. What was the matter with him? What did he want? I could have killed that man, and all I did was to shoot him in the foot. She imagined herself as Tosca, Adam as Cavaradossi, singing an aria to the sweet little hand of hers that had dealt the death blow to his enemy. Evidently she was not supposed to behave like an opera heroine. Or she and Adam hadn't seen the same operas. *A very dangerous woman.* Well, maybe she was. Maybe Adam just didn't appreciate her better qualities.

When the company gathered in the stable

yard Holbert Bruns appeared among them, transformed by the genius of stage veteran Robert Montmorency-Chalmers into a pretty good approximation of Big Ed Strawfield. "Down with the capitalists," he said, and laughed.

Adam was so impressed with the transformation that he changed the shooting schedule again. "I want a low-angle close-up of Strawfield delivering a labor speech," he said to Mr. Johnson. "Shoot it now, while his makeup still looks this good. Emily tells me you have a new lens for close-up work. I want nothing appearing behind him but those wispy clouds blowing past. Can you do that?"

"Yep," Johnson said. "Just give me a minute." He fished a piece of orange-colored glass out of his kit and fastened it over the close-up lens. "This will bring up the clouds," he explained to Billy Parker, who was watching him with the rapt attention of an apprentice.

"How many feet of film did you shoot at the railway station yesterday?" Adam said.

"Plenty," Johnson said. "Lots of folks got off the train. Some even looked like they might be Westerners. You can pick and choose, cut what you like."

"Good. Here, Mr. Bruns, get up on this

box. Now shake your fist in the air and give us a good labor speech."

It went well. Mr. Bruns had heard a number of labor speeches when he was working undercover for the Pinkertons, and he had the rhythm and the rhetoric. Shooting upward at an angle past Mr. Bruns's padded belly, Johnson got several minutes of fist-shaking, palm-pounding, capitalist-damning speechifying before Adam called, "Cut!"

"That was good," Emily said to Mr. Bruns. "Almost as if you had real acting experience. What will your wife think, when you tell her you're in the movies?"

"Lydia likes movies," Mr. Bruns said, with a chuckle. "I'm sure she'll be very pleased."

"And your children. How many did you say you had again?"

"Three. Two. We plan on having more."

"You and Lydia."

"Yes." He looked at her straight-faced, once more the tame Great Dane. Did he even have a wife? Was he not, in fact, still working for the Pinkertons, or maybe for Thomas Edison himself? Maybe it was Holbert Bruns who set the Actophone studio on fire, and not McCoy at all. She should have told Adam who he was.

"Places, everybody!" Adam called. "Places

for the riot scene!" Emily shivered. Last time they staged a riot somebody wound up dead. Was she wanted in the scene? Probably not; she wasn't in makeup. Her eye would look very bad.

Adam was still treating her coldly, still angry because she shot Grogan. Maybe he would sooner she lay there and let the man break all her ribs. Maybe he thought little Fay was a more womanly sort of person, using her wiles to make things go her way. That's what I need, she thought. Wiles. I need to be wily. Then I would get around the men and they would never notice I was doing it. Like a real woman.

Again Adam and Mr. Johnson conferred about camera angles. Although the bread man showed up promptly at eight thirty, ready to go to work, and Fred and Billy Parker straggled in at eight thirty-five with their clothes all smoky, very few actors were there to represent the huge riotous mob. Erno, as Oskar Heikkinen, must appear to be leading a mob of strikers — that would be Fred, Billy, and the bread man, who called himself Albert Brown — against Boss Bohnert — that would be Chalmers — with Big Ed on one side of him, and Mrs. Heikkinen, with the baby in her arms, on the other side. The part of the baby would be played by a rolled-up hotel towel.

Moving the camera during filming was out of the question, Mr. Johnson said, but there was a breeze to move Fay's hair, if they positioned the actors just right. Where was Fay, anyway?

"Has anyone seen Fay?" Adam said. They all shook their heads. He put his megaphone to his lips and bellowed, in the general direction of the hotel: "Fay Winningly! Places!"

No answer.

"Emily, go find out what happened to Fay, will you? Tell her to get herself down here. And while you're there put some makeup over that eye. I'm going to need you for the crowd scene."

Emily went into the hotel and up the stairs. "Fay!" she called. No answer. A sound of stealthy movement came from the women's dressing room, whose door was slightly ajar. "Fay?"

Fay's street clothes lay crumpled on the bed. On the vanity table a rat left off chewing a stick of Fay's greasepaint and stared at Emily insolently.

"Scat!" Emily threw her shoe at it and the thing scuttled through a hole in the wood-work.

She sat down in front of the dressing-table

mirror. I look terrible, she thought. I look as if someone had beaten me up, as if I hadn't slept in days on top of that. Which he did, and I haven't. Over a foundation of cold cream she began to paint her eye. Rats in the makeup. Yet another disagreeable thing to force back into the dark corners of her mind. Maybe Mrs. Potts had some more Fernet-Branca.

Where was Fay?

Outside, Adam called her again through the megaphone.

Perhaps she ran away. Seeing Adam was free, not knowing Big Ed had confessed to the murder, perhaps Fay thought her crime had been discovered, and sneaked back to Manhattan before Chief Watson could take her and put her in jail. But, leaving her makeup behind?

Emily stood up and turned to go back outside, and it was then that she saw Fay's prairie housewife costume, bonnet and all, hanging on a hook on the back of the door.

"Fay!" she called. Perhaps the girl was in the bathroom. Emily went down the hall to look. The bathroom door was shut. A shadow moved behind the frosted glass. "Fay?"

"No, ma'am, it's me," Mary Grace said, opening the door a crack. "I'm cleaning the tub in here."

"Have you seen Miss Winningly?"

"No, ma'am, I haven't."

Emily went back down the hallway toward the stairs. On a whim, she knocked on the linen closet door. "Fay? Are you in there?" Of course she wasn't in there; all the men were outside in the stable yard. There wouldn't be any point.

And yet, like Bluebeard's wife, Emily found herself opening the closet door.

Fay's lifeless body lay propped against the bottom shelf in her bust bodice and petticoat, her eyes wide, her mouth open. The base of a bill spindle protruded from beneath her left breast. There was very little blood. She must have died instantly. How long had she been lying there? Emily touched her hand. It was cold, the hand of a dead person. *"Oh, thou weed."*

Behind her, a rustle of skirts, and then Mary Grace started screaming again.

Twenty-One

Shortly after Mary Grace stopped screaming Chief Watson arrived with his boys in
blue and a horse-drawn ambulance. The
chief took a cursory look at the scene in the
linen closet and then made all the actors
and hotel people line up on the front porch.

"You know, making these pictures of yours
is a commercial activity," he said, glaring at
Adam. "I'm starting to think you need a
license for that, and if any more murders
happen here I'll make damn sure you don't
ever get one. You'll never make another
movie in Fort Lee." His two men trudged
past them and down the steps, carrying
Fay's slim little body on a stretcher, covered
with a hotel sheet. A stray golden sausage
curl hung over the side. Emily caught a
whiff of the dead actress's lily of the valley
cologne. Mary Grace was still weeping.

The chief looked around at the rest of the
assembled crowd. "I want all your names

and addresses, and I want all of you to make yourselves available for questioning later. Nobody leave town." Back to Adam. "So. Mr. and Mrs. Weiss. Knickerbocker Hotel in Manhattan. Is that right?"

"Yes," Adam said.

"I'll talk to you later." He waved his hand, dismissing them. "Next."

They went inside. Adam stood staring at the fire with his hands in his back pockets. Through the windows they could hear Watson questioning the actors, their murmured responses, then the slow clopping of horses' hooves and the creaking of the ambulance as it started down the road.

Adam sighed and said, "Well, Emily, at least we got a break."

"What break?" Emily said.

"The prairie housewife costume. If Fay had been killed wearing it we would have to find another one."

"And who's going to wear the one she left behind?"

"You are. You'll have to play Mrs. Heikkinen."

"Me?"

"Come now, you're a trained actress, aren't you? Weren't you on the stage when we met?"

"Adam, look at me. My eye is swollen

shut. My ribs are so bruised I can hardly breathe. I can't do this."

He took her by the shoulders. "And what are you going to tell our grandchildren? That you threw away their chances in life because you had a few bruises?"

"What if I fall off the cliff? Where will our grandchildren come from then?"

"Sweetheart, you won't fall."

"All right, then, what if the murderer pushes me?"

"What murderer?"

"Adam, Adam, two people have been killed. Somebody here did it." She waved her hand at the actors outside the window, now milling around in the stable yard like restless cattle.

"Nonsense. It was probably a passing vagrant. You'll be safe as long as I'm looking after you. Run along upstairs and get into your costume and makeup."

"Can't we at least cut out the scenes on the cliff?"

"Sweetheart, there isn't time. Run along, now, like a good girl. Hurry while we still have the light. We'll shoot the close-ups on your good profile. You'll do fine."

Emily began to suspect once again that Adam was losing his mind. Two stabbing deaths in a week, and only Emily seemed to think it important to find out who the murderer might be. Unless Chief Watson really thought it was important. He didn't, though, did he? He already knew. It was him.

Or possibly it wasn't.

When Emily went outside in her makeup and costume Watson was gone. Adam was reassuring the cast and crew in tones of deep sincerity that the show would go on. Some seemed pleased at the going on of the show. Others were offended. Erno Berg remained as wooden as ever. Billy and Fred were uneasy about continuing to work on the very day that Fay had met her death. They said it didn't seem right to them; maybe it was because they were Mohawks, they said. Mohawks had feelings about death.

Adam pointed out to them that in their former sphere the death of a worker or two never stopped a bridge from getting built.

"Well, yeah, it did," Billy said. "They still haven't finished the Quebec bridge that fell down that time."

"Because of engineering problems," Fred said, "not because of all those people dying."

"That's what *they* say. Me, I think different."

"It'll be fine, boys," Adam said. "Just get to work. Don't worry about a thing."

Robert Montmorency-Chalmers, like the old trouper he was, was ready to do his scenery-chewing duty no matter who died. Or who he killed, Emily reflected. His behavior never changed, no matter what was going on around him. In front of the camera he was manic. Behind the scenes he was consistently morose. Of all the people who might have stabbed poor little Fay to death, Chalmers was the least likely to let it show on his face. He could easily do murder and never betray himself by the smallest alteration in his manner. It was just as he said; he was the only real actor in the company.

Aside from Emily herself, that is. In her prairie dress, makeup, and curly blond wig Emily found that she was able to get completely into character and forget everything other than the story she was portraying, forget her questions about which of her associates might be the guilty party in the murders, even forget that Adam was going to require her to play the last few scenes on the edge of the dreaded cliff.

By the time the red sun went down behind the smoky horizon *Massacre at Bitter Wash* was all but finished. Only three scenes remained to be filmed: the terrifying climax on the cliff side, the rescue, and the final clinch. A clinch scene with the wooden Erno could scarcely be imagined, but Emily expected to be able to improvise something for Mr. Johnson to get on film.

The day's shooting had gone so well that Adam and Emily made up their quarrel somehow and laughed together on the ferry. After tomorrow there would be time to cry for the dead, time for Emily to explain to Adam about her height fear, time to sort out how Fay and Duffy had met their death and at whose hands, but tonight they were determined to be merry. Adam chuckled as he passed through the subway door marked "Knickerbocker," smiled as he ordered two of the fashionable new gin drinks from bartender Martini, grinned and pinched Emily's bottom on their way up in the elevator. A good hot bath and a soft warm bed awaited them.

When he opened the door all his merriment fell away.

"What has happened here?"

It almost seemed as though the chambermaid had neglected to clean up after Emily's tussle with Grogan. Not only were the bullet hole and the bloodstain from Grogan's foot still there in the carpet but all the drawers, the bedclothes, and the mattress had been dumped on the floor again. Emily rushed to the bathroom. At least the chemicals, the cans of spare film, and the various photographic paraphernalia were still neatly in their places.

"Take a bath, Adam," she said. "I'll deal with all this."

"I'll be damned if I will," Adam said. "Where is that chambermaid?"

"She must have neglected —"

"Look at this mess! What's missing? Are your jewels still here?"

"We sold them, darling, don't you remember?" The bottom drawer of the bureau lay upside down at her feet. She turned it over. Nothing was underneath. "Mr. Duffy's blackmail files are gone," she said.

"Do we need them?"

"No."

"Then I'll go and bathe. Get the chambermaid to see about this."

Emily put her head out the door and caught Bessie, the chambermaid, as she trundled her cart down the hall on the last pass of her sixteen-hour shift. "Can you come in here, please?"

"I didn't tell the bosses what you was doing in the bathroom."

"No, but you let someone in, didn't you?"

"Me?"

281

"A tall, thin man?" Bessie shook her head. "Or a short, dark-haired man with a bandaged foot and a limp?"

Bessie began to cry.

"It's all right, it's no use crying over spilled milk."

She sniffled. "He spilled milk in there?"

"No, only shirtwaists and underwear. Come in and help me pick the room up."

The chambermaid was aghast at the wreckage. "He say he just want to look."

"He looked, all right. Oh, stop that crying before you get me started."

"I feel bad."

"Let's just pick it up."

"He give me a dollar. I wouldn't of took it except my babies needs shoes."

"Spare me. You sound like Holbert Bruns."

"Who?"

"A man I know."

"Oh. Is anything stole?"

"Nothing valuable." She picked up a stack of Adam's custom-made shirts and tucked them into the top bureau drawer. "Actually we haven't got anything valuable."

Between the two of them the women got the mattress back on the bed, the drawers back in the chest, the clothes back in the drawers. Bessie made the bed up with fresh sheets. By the time Adam emerged from the bathroom, draped in a large Turkish towel, the room was all in order.

Bessie lunged for the door. "Just a minute," Adam said.

"Yes, sir?"

"Bring me some sandwiches from the kitchen, will you? Black bread, pastrami, and cheese, with some good English mustard and a couple of bottles of celery tonic. I don't expect to be billed for it."

"No, sir." She rushed away down the hall.

"Not billed for it?" Emily said.

"Sweetheart, the woman owes us something. Let her steal us some supper."

"I feel as though I were sinking into a slough of corruption."

"What's the matter with you now?"

"Corruption. We might have known that if we could bribe Bessie not to say anything to the management about our running a film lab in the bathroom then Grogan could bribe her to let him into our room. It's what happens when you lend yourself to this sort of thing."

"Bushwah. He offered her money. She took it. The woman needs money. Everybody needs money."

"It's corruption. It's sneaking around. Today it's hiding the lab from the hotel management, tomorrow it's suborning the help to steal food from the kitchen. We should have rented an office to develop our film, where we could have done it honestly in the clear light of day."

"There speaks a New En gland Puritan," Adam said. "The clear light of day would have ruined the film. To say nothing of exposing us to Edison and the Trust." He tried to take her in his arms; she pushed him away. "There, there, sweetheart, hang on. Don't lose your nerve now. We're so close. When we finish this picture tomorrow and get the copies into Howie Kazanow's hands we'll have the money to build a whole studio where we can do whatever we want. We'll hire enough lawyers to tie Thomas Edison in knots."

"And the murders?"

"Be damned to the murders. Worry about them the day after tomorrow."

"You really don't mind that we have someone in our midst killing people. That's two people now. These things tend to run in threes. Who's next? What if it's you? What if it's me?"

"Your fears are irrational, Emily. No one wants to kill us. Just think of this: Melpomene Moving Picture Studios, all-powerful purveyor of entertainment to the

American public. We can make it happen tomorrow."

Twenty-Two

"Mrs. Weiss, do you want me to nail this to a tree?" Fred said, brandishing the new Melpomene trademark he had whittled out of a piece of stove wood. "The ground is frozen too hard to stick it in anywhere, and the rocks by the cliff don't seem to have any cracks the right size."

Freshly made up, carefully bewigged and costumed, Emily stood within three feet of the edge of the precipice, looking down. What Adam had told her was true; it was not a sheer drop to the rocky banks of the Hudson far below. There was, in fact, a ledge down there about a foot wide, maybe eight or nine feet from the top of the cliff. She rubbed her hands together. Her fingers were going numb, and not from cold. "Where's Mr. Weiss?" she said.

"In the hotel talking to the actors."

"Then ask Mr. Johnson about it. He'll know where to put the trademark so that it shows up the best." She stepped away from the edge again and tried to control her breathing, in, out, in, out. What would Vera have done? Were there any techniques in the arsenal of Mr. Stanislavsky to help her get through the next few hours? She kept seeing herself falling, arms flailing helplessly, bonnet strings streaming out in the wind. *Try to concentrate on something else.*

Adam, for example. What a handsome man. Here he came down the steps of the hotel, shaved, bathed, elegantly shod, complete with new shoelaces, his Norfolk jacket steamed and pressed until you'd never guess it had been his pillow for a long week in Chief Watson's lice-ridden jailhouse. His megaphone and folding chair were under his arm, ready for work.

"Put the trademark anywhere you can, Fred, there's a good fellow. And get Billy to make us a fire. Have him put the fire barrel next to the cliff, but out of the way of the camera. Now, then. Mr. Johnson. What's the best angle for this? I want a sense of the vastness of space out beyond the cliff, but not any of the New York skyline."

"Naturally," Mr. Johnson said. "I have it all worked out."

"Good. Emily, I want you out on the very lip of that cliff, maybe slipping a little. Can we do a close-up of loose rocks, Mr. Johnson, coming loose and falling into the abyss?"

"I can get that for you. For the rest, it will take another hour and a half for the sun to come around to where the light is just right."

"Fine, that'll give us plenty of time to get the costumes and makeup fixed. We'll cut back and forth between the falling rocks and Emily's fingers slipping. Sweetheart, I think you need more rouge on your cheeks. They're awfully pale."

"When you say, my fingers slipping, Adam, you mean . . ."

"Now, Chalmers, you're after Emily. As far as you're aware she's defenseless. Stroke that mustache. I want to see the whites around your eyes."

"How far out on the cliff are we going to play this?" Chalmers said.

"All the way out, where that yellow string is set up, see it? Don't worry, it's perfectly safe. There's a ledge before you get to the thousand-foot drop."

"Is Mrs. Potts in the kitchen?" Emily said.

"Why?" Adam said.

"I think I'd like a little more of that drink she gave me."

"Don't be silly, sweetheart, the sun isn't over the yardarm yet. Ah, good, here comes

Erno. Erno, where's your blood?"

"My blood?"

"Your shirt is supposed to be all torn and bloody. Don't you remember? You got shot yesterday."

"Oh."

"Emily, take him inside and make him up properly. And put some rouge on yourself, sweetheart. You look ghastly."

"Right, chief."

She went back up to the dressing room with Erno and painted his eyes and lips while he sat like the block of wood he was. "Now, Erno, since you've just been in a fight your hair must be messy. Let me just put —" She worked some brilliantine into his locks and ruffled them until they were attractively disheveled. "That's good. Now you need some blood on that shirt," she said. "And it ought to be torn. Give it to me; I'll fix it." He stripped off his shirt and handed it over.

In the flesh under his right rib there was a round, puckered scar, and another on the side of his back. "Heavens, Erno, that scar almost looks like a bullet hole. How did you get that?"

"That's my business," he said.

"I'm sorry. Of course it is." That would be the bullet wound Adam mentioned, the one

Fay had teased him about. Probably the result of some embarrassing childhood stunt. She ripped the shirt collar and dribbled some false blood on the front of the shirt. "Here you are. Mr. Weiss doesn't need us for another hour or so. I'll see you outside." He went out of the dressing room and down the stairs, buttoning up his shirt.

Or not the result of a stunt. Maybe Erno's scar was something significant. Maybe it was a clue. Emily's money was still on Francis X. Watson for the murders, but they might just as easily have been done by some member of the movie company, Erno for reasons of his own, Robert Montmorency-Chalmers defending himself from a blackmailer, then killing Fay in a fit of jealousy, even Mr. Johnson, or the Indians. People said that Mohawks could be murdering rascals. Look how they all carried knives. Or the Pinkertons, treacherous thieves and liars that they were. She painted over the purple eye again, powdered her face, and beaded her eyelashes.

When her makeup was adjusted to what she hoped would be Adam's satisfaction, Emily went downstairs to find Mrs. Potts and a fortifying snort of her favorite tipple. Holbert Bruns was sitting in Mr. Potts's chair by the fire, with his feet stretched out on Mr. Potts's leather ottoman. Since his back was to the stairs Emily thought to sneak out to the kitchen without being noticed. It was not to be.

Without turning his head, Holbert Bruns said, "Tell me why you mentioned the name of Jack Simpkins, Mrs. Weiss."

"Oh. That." She came into the lobby. No point in avoiding this discussion. In any case it would take her mind off the scene she had to play on the cliff outside.

"Did Seamus Duffy mention Simpkins in his memoir?"

"I don't know. I didn't read the whole thing."

"Then what made you say —"

"He wrote that he was going to talk about Governor Frank Steunenberg's murder, and then he began to lead up to it, saying that he went to Caldwell with Harry Orchard and Steve Adams. I stopped reading right after he asked some loafer at the train station where Frank Steunenberg lived."

"So?"

"It was my understanding that the three men who went to Caldwell to murder Frank Steunenberg were Harry Orchard, Steve Adams, and Jack Simpkins. Simpkins was never captured. Some said he was a Pinkerton provocateur. Why wouldn't Simpkins be a name that Duffy used?"

"Why, indeed? But he didn't say that, in the memoir."

"He might have."

"Wouldn't you like to know for certain?"

"Yes. As a matter of fact, I would."

"Let's go, then."

"Where?"

"To the Fort Lee police station." He sprang up, took her arm, and propelled her irresistibly out the front door. "We'll make Chief Watson give you the memoirs back."

Francis X. Watson was writing up some sort of report when Emily and Holbert Bruns burst into his office. He covered the work hastily and glared at them.

"Chief Watson. Do you have a moment?" Emily said.

"No," Watson said. "What do you want?" The stick pen in his hand was dripping splotches of blue ink.

Emily glanced at Bruns. This was his plan, after all. How was he going to recover the memoirs? "Chief Watson, my name is Holbert Bruns. I understand that Mrs. Weiss, here, gave you something of great interest to my employers."

"You're working for Mr. and Mrs. Weiss, ain't you?"

"I am, but I'm also in the employ of the Pinkerton National Detective Agency."

"Ah."

"Mr. Seamus Duffy used to work for them, too, years ago."

"I know that," Chief Watson said.

"You know because you have his memoirs that I gave you," Emily said.

"Yep. Evidence in a murder investigation."

"Evidence, yes, but not crucial evidence," Bruns said.

"Where do you get that idea?"

"You don't need Mr. Duffy's memoirs to prove your case. Mrs. Weiss also gave you a signed confession from Mr. Edward Strawfield to Mr. Duffy's murder."

"True."

"Which makes the memoirs unnecessary. Am I right?"

"I s'pose so. But the background information —"

"The background information can be found in back issues of any big-city newspaper. But Mr. Duffy's memoirs also contain material that might be embarrassing to the Pinkerton agency. And speaking of embarrassment —" Bruns reached inside his jacket. For an instant Emily thought this man meant to draw his gun and stick up the police chief, making her an accessory to a felony. Unless he shot him dead, and then she would merely be a murder witness. But, no, Bruns put his hand in some inner pocket and withdrew a small, tattered brown notebook. The Big Mitt Ledger. He must have gotten it from Grogan, who was still with the Pinkertons, just as she thought. "I believe this is yours, sir."

"No, it ain't."

"Your initials are F.W. You won't deny that, I'm sure."

"You two get out of my office."

"It was sad about Miss Winningly, don't you agree?"

"What did you say your name was again?"

"My name is Bruns, sir. You must admit it looks bad for Fort Lee, two murders in a week. Bad for the town's reputation." Bruns slipped the Big Mitt Ledger back into the pocket of his coat. "Bad for your reputation, too."

Chief Watson put down the pen, making a blot of ink on the desk alongside the other blots, and opened his desk drawer. Emily caught sight of a nickel-plated revolver where it lay gleaming among the gum erasers, sticks of sealing wax, and rubber bands. "Get out of here," he said again. She tugged at the detective's sleeve.

Ignoring her, Bruns coolly withdrew

another item from his pocket, Duffy's penciled note. He read from it: " 'Received telephone message from F.W. — filming resumes today.' F.W. is Francis Watson, isn't it, Chief, telling Duffy everything Melpomene did? Duffy used the boodle diary, your Big Mitt Ledger, to force you to help him keep track of the movie people."

"You betrayed us to Thomas Edison's detectives, didn't you?" Emily said. "We knew it was you. I must say I thought your behavior quite shabby." Peck him to death, that's right. Then he'll be sure to give up the memoirs.

Chief Watson's fingers closed around the gun, then opened again and moved to a package of chewing tobacco. He took it out of the drawer and broke off a plug.

As Bruns put the note back in his pocket he let his coat hang open far enough to allow Chief Watson to see his own gun, snug in its shoulder holster. "We know that Big Ed Strawfield was in Russia when Fay Winningly was killed," he went on, sounding more and more like a courtroom lawyer. "He couldn't have committed both murders, I'm sure you'll agree."

"Maybe you killed Miss Winningly, Bruns. Or you, Mrs. Weiss. Maybe you both killed her because she knew too much about the death of Duffy." Chief Watson closed the desk drawer and sat stolidly masticating his Mail Pouch.

"I have the death of Duffy on film," Emily said.

"Do you, now?" Holbert Bruns said.

"You can clearly see" — she began, watching carefully for any reaction from Chief Watson; alas, there was none — "that neither Mr. Bruns nor I was anywhere near Duffy when he was killed. You were right on the spot, though, Chief Watson, weren't you?"

"Me and twenty other people," the chief grumbled. "I still think Mr. Weiss did it, if it wasn't Big Ed Strawfield."

How disappointing to see that the chief wasn't acting the least bit guilty, at least not guilty of murder. His reaction to the sight of the Big Mitt Ledger was gratifying — now that was guilt written all over him — and he jumped very furtively to cover up the papers he was working on when she and Holbert Bruns came into his office. But when Emily hinted that she might have a moving picture of him killing Duffy he exhibited no reaction at all, not a tic, not a tremor. So it wasn't him.

Bruns said, "I think you'll find the killer was another one of those twenty people."

Clearly this must be the case, Emily thought. Another one of the twenty. But who?

The chief said, "Do tell."

"Someone who was being blackmailed by Duffy," Bruns said. "Other than you I mean, Chief. Someone whose advances the lovely Miss Winningly had spurned. Of course, if you don't want to see my evidence, I'll be going now. It's been a long day. Mrs. Weiss has a movie to make and I have people to see."

"Just a minute. What evidence? And who says Duffy was blackmailing me?"

"Duffy kept files on people," Emily said.

"Fay Winningly for one," Bruns said. "You for another, as we see by the ledger here." He took it out and waggled it at the chief.

"I told you that ain't mine."

"Another was Robert Montmorency."

"Who?"

"Mr. Chalmers," Emily said. *Oh, thou weed.* Suddenly it made perfect sense. The drug-crazed assassin. The jealous lover. The man Emily was going to have to go out and play a scene with on the edge of a thousand-foot cliff, in about — she glanced at the wall clock — fifteen minutes.

"Oh. Him," the chief said. "But what —"

"Here." From yet another pocket Bruns

produced that strange five-by-eight sepia tone picture of Montmorency in the opium den. "Here is the evidence that Duffy held over Montmorency's head." Chief Watson put out his hand to take it, but Bruns pulled it back out of his reach. "As you're not interested, I guess I'll be forced to go back to the Pinkerton Agency and tell my superiors —"

"No, hold up, hold up. I've got an idea."

"Have you?"

"How about I give you Duffy's book, and you give me the ledger and the evidence against Mr. Robert Chalmers."

"Montmorency," Bruns said.

"Who?"

"Robert Montmorency. That's Mr. Chalmers's real name. It's written on the back of the photograph, in case you need to know how to spell it."

Chief Watson opened his desk drawer again and for a heartbeat his hand hovered over his service revolver. This was a man used to having his own way, Emily reflected. Bruns had got the better of him in front of a witness. What if he shot them both and told people they had been killed trying to escape? Stranger things had happened. But instead he sighed and pulled out the manila envelope holding the memoirs. "Here's Duffy's book," he said. "What do you say to a trade?"

"It's a deal," Bruns said. "I'm glad you thought of this way of handling things, Chief Watson." With a grunt the chief handed over the manuscript and took the Big Mitt Ledger, the penciled note, and the picture of Robert Montmorency-Chalmers dozing on drugs. If he had thought to ask, he could have gotten some money, too. Weren't the Pinkertons prepared to pay a thousand dollars for Duffy's book? Now they could have it for free. But not before Emily read it.

"Let me see the manuscript," Emily said to Bruns as the two of them headed for the hotel.

"We'll both have a look at it, sweetheart."

"Don't call me sweetheart. Give me the manuscript." He made no move to do so. As they approached the hotel Adam was sitting on the front porch, reading over the scenario. Oh, Lord, it was almost time to do the scene.

Of course, she could go to Adam and say, Chalmers is the killer. You can't possibly send him out on that cliff to play a scene with me. He'll throw me to my death. Adam would point out that Chalmers had no reason to throw her to her death. She wasn't

299

any threat to him.

But if she was some threat to him, then what? The thing that frightened her even more than falling or being thrown off the cliff was that Adam, given a choice between finishing the picture and saving her life, would choose to finish the picture. When she found that out for certain she would have to leave him. It would be horribly painful, not to mention the inconvenience. Her mother would say, "I told you so."

Feeling that an unpleasant confrontation with Adam was coming, unwilling to get into it right then, she said to Bruns, "Let's go around back." Maybe Adam wouldn't see them.

Her attempt to escape Adam's notice was in vain. "Ten minutes, Emily," he called after her, without looking up. She gave him no answer, but continued on her way to the kitchen door.

Mrs. Potts was peeling potatoes at the table when Emily and Bruns came into the hotel kitchen. Bruns greeted her warmly, like one who was quite at home, and made a place on the table for Duffy's manuscript among the potato peelings.

"Let me see it," Emily said. "Let me find out the answer to one question, at least, before I die."

"You're not going to die," Bruns said. He stepped aside and let her look. She began to leaf through it, searching for the place where she had left off.

"Die! I should think not," Mrs. Potts said.

"Mrs. Potts, I wonder if you have any more of that drink that's so good for an upset stomach," Emily said.

"For height fear, you mean," Mrs. Potts said. "Haven't you told Mr. Weiss yet how frightened you are of heights?"

"No."

"That's a sin. Look at you. Look at her, Mr. Bruns."

"I am. I'm looking at her."

Emily closed the manuscript. "I have to do the scene," she said, as though that explained anything. "I have to. It's important for the picture. I just need a little something to help me get through it."

"Well, then, I'll go down cellar and get you what you want." Mrs. Potts put down the paring knife and wiped her hands on the roller towel on the back of the cellar door. "But, remember, I advised against it. Your husband ought to get somebody else." She opened the door to the dark cellar. A moldy smell came out, and she went down into it.

Under his breath Bruns said something

301

that sounded like, "Or you ought to get another husband."

"What did you say?"

"Mrs. Weiss, look at yourself. Your eye is almost swollen shut. You're trembling. You can hardly take a breath for the injury to your ribs."

"Oh. Well, I —"

"And you're still the most beautiful creature I've ever seen."

"Mr. Bruns!"

"Listen to me. You don't have to do this."

"I don't?"

"You don't. The world won't come to an end if you turn your back on that cliff and just walk away."

Holbert Bruns was so close that she could smell his coat again, and him inside it, and also a trace of tobacco from a pipe that she had never yet seen him smoke. He touched her shoulder, and she let him, not shrinking from his hand. This was highly unusual, Emily suffering men to rest their hands on parts of her person. She remembered distinctly the first time it had happened with Adam. He was slipping a mink coat around her shoulder. It was not the monetary value of the fur that had conquered her, but rather Adam's easy assumption that he knew what she needed, and he had it to give her.

302

Maybe that wasn't true anymore. "Just walk away," she repeated.

"With me. Walk away with me. I'll take you somewhere perfectly flat. I'll take you to Grand Island, Nebraska. We'll walk hand in hand along the banks of the perfectly flat Platte River. You'll never crawl out on another precipice. I'll take you to meet my mother. I'll marry you. I'll take care of you the way you deserve to be taken care of."

"But you're already married. What about those towheaded little boys?"

"That was a story I made up, the wife, the little boys. A picture I bought from a studio."

"Well, *I'm* married. What about Adam?"

"Adam Weiss has no idea of your value. No idea what he has. You're the most wonderful —" His lips were on her neck.

"Mr. Bruns, I must ask you to stop that."

"Come with me, Emily. Come away from all this. Adam doesn't appreciate you. He doesn't deserve you. I love you. I've never known anybody like you."

He wasn't beautiful, the way Adam was, and yet he had some quality that was so . . . "It's really flat in Grand Island?"

"It's the prairie, darling. You'll never see anyplace flatter."

Mrs. Potts came clumping up the cellar stairs. Emily stepped backward, disentangling herself. As Mrs. Potts poured her a jelly glass full of thick green liquid Emily looked at herself in the mirror over the sink. It was not true that her eye was swollen shut. Maybe none of the rest of it was true, either. Mrs. Potts handed her the potion; she quaffed it down. Under the makeup the color began to come back to her cheeks.

"You should make him get another actress," Mrs. Potts said. "Right away, dear, before something bad happens." She bustled away in the direction of the parlor.

Emily heaved a long sigh. "It won't do," she said.

"What won't?" Holbert Bruns approached her again, but she moved to put the kitchen table between herself and his deadly aura.

"Running off to Nebraska. I want to thank you for your kind offer, Mr. Bruns, it means more to me than you'll ever know, but I love my husband. Whether he appreciates me or not. And I have to do this thing on the cliff; my mother didn't raise me to be a quitter." She put the empty jelly glass down on the table. "Here I go."

"Just the same, one of these days you're going to take a good look at this man who sends you out to do dangerous stunts, all banged up the way you are, and you're going to notice that he's not good enough for you."

"He is. He's good enough for me."

"He's not, and you're going to see it one day. And when you do I'll still be around. Good luck, my dearest Emily. *Au revoir.*"

TWENTY-THREE

Adam and Angus Johnson huddled around the fire barrel, drinking the last of Fred Parker's bitter coffee. It was time to do the scene.

"McCoy is in town, boss," Johnson said.

"Who?" Adam said.

"Edison's man. Fred and Billy overheard him talking on the pay phone to Edison just now in the soda shop."

"Does he know we're filming here today?" The sun had finally reached the optimum angle for filming the scene. The last thing Melpomene needed was for the hated McCoy to show up and spoil the production.

"I guess he does. On the phone he was talking about burning down the Actophone studio. Told Edison it was an accident."

"Good Lord."

"We're ready for him, Mr. Weiss," Billy said, and handed Johnson a cinnamon bun.

"More or less," Johnson said. "Keep an

eye out for him, anyway."

"What are you doing?" Adam said. Billy had put a sticky cinnamon bun in his gloved hand.

"Might as well eat 'em," Billy said. "They're good. We needed to clear some space in the bread truck."

"For what?"

"Oh, we thought —"

"Never mind," Adam said. Billy's weird Mohawk ideas about movie production were more than he wanted to deal with just then, with McCoy getting ready to swoop down on them at any moment. As Billy went back in the bread truck, probably looking for more to eat, Adam asked Johnson whether the camera was all warmed up.

"Yep," Johnson said.

"Is Emily in place?"

"All the actors are in place," Johnson said. "Everything is in place." Chalmers and Emily were on their marks at the edge of the cliff.

"All right then." Adam unfolded his chair and set it squarely behind Mr. Johnson and his camera. "Roll film. Action!" He liked the raspy authoritative sound his voice made when he projected it through the megaphone. Like the fresh shine on his shoes, it seemed to affirm some quality in himself that he admired but could not name, perhaps the quality of being an important director.

And then he felt a hand on his shoulder. Chief Francis X. Watson was standing over him with two stalwart rustics in uniform.

"What now? Can't you see we're trying to make a picture here?"

"Hate to interrupt," the chief said, "but it's police business."

Adam got up, left his chair and his megaphone, and walked with the chief and his men toward the street, away from the scene of the shooting. The cast knew what to do. Johnson knew what to do. What was needed now was to keep these people away from them.

"I'm looking for Mr. Montmorency," the chief said. "Is that him over there in the plutocrat suit?" The real J. J. Bohnert would never have worn dinner clothes and an ersatz diamond stickpin at that hour of the afternoon, still less to attend riots and pursue helpless young housewives, but the public expected its millionaires to dress like that on-screen. Melpomene's wardrobe department — which is to say, Emily — happily obliged.

"Yes, that's him," Adam said. "He's shooting the last scene of this movie. What do you want him for?"

"Me and the boys are here to arrest him for the murder of Seamus Duffy and Fay Winningly."

Chalmers? "What makes you think he's guilty?"

"I got an open-and-shut case against him. Pinkerton man helped me out on this one, I ain't ashamed to say so. There's many a law enforcement agent owes the Pinkertons a debt of gratitude."

"What Pinkerton man?"

"Mr. Holbert Bruns."

"He's not a detective, he's an actor."

"A man of parts," the chief said.

"Evidently." Out of the tail of his eye Adam could see the work on his picture proceeding apace. *Stall, Weiss. Stall. Maybe you can get the picture finished before this moron arrests your last actor.* "How did Mr. Bruns help you, if you don't mind my asking?"

"I don't suppose it can do any harm to tell you, Mr. Weiss. Mr. Bruns turned over a key piece of evidence in the case. Seamus Duffy was a blackmailer."

"You astonish me."

"No, it's true. Mr. Duffy was blackmailing Mr. Montmorency with evidence of gross moral turpitude; Montmorency saw his chance, and killed him; as for the young lady, I understand that she threw Mr. Montmorency over for another man in the cast. He stabbed her to death in a fit of jealousy."

"I see. But the evidence you spoke of —"

"Right here." The chief took a photograph out of his pocket. "As this picture clearly demonstrates, your Mr. Montmorency is nothing but a dope fiend." He held it out for Adam's inspection. There lay Robert Montmorency on a mean and greasy cot, his eyes rolled up, his tongue lolling out, his hand extended to accept a pipe held out to him by long-nailed fingers protruding from a hokey Chinese sleeve embroidered with dragons. In the lower left-hand corner, in tiny letters, were the words *Edison Studios.*

"This is a lobby card," Adam said.

"A what?"

"This is a still from the worst moving picture ever made, *Secrets of an Opium Fiend.* A product of the Edison Studios, as it says right here. This picture ran in my nickelodeons for barely half a day before the audiences began throwing rotten fruit at the screen. We had a devil of a time cleaning it up. So that's where I've seen Montmorency's face before!"

"A movie?"

"A movie. A very bad movie. Maybe

310

Montmorency would kill to keep people from being reminded of it. I would be tempted to, myself, if I were associated with that picture. But it seems so unlikely."

"That's your story, Mr. Weiss. I say the man is a dope fiend and a murderer, and I mean to arrest him at once and bring him to trial as soon as the judge gets back from Florida."

"You're making another mistake."

Watson looked at Adam for a long time with narrowed eyes. "Well, somebody did it," he said at last. "If it wasn't Montmorency, maybe I was right all along and it was you." He took out a plug of chewing tobacco and bit off a chunk. "Did you read that article I gave you about the electric chair? It was interesting. They say you can smell your own flesh cooking."

Thank you, Mr. Edison, for the onward march of civilization. The fillings in Adam's molars tingled electrically. "Can you at least wait until we finish filming this scene?"

"No."

"Go get him, then, if you can," Adam said, gesturing toward the cliff. "Just be careful not to let him hurt my wife."

Hanging by her fingers from the edge of the precipice under the pitiless eye of Mr.

311

Johnson's camera, Emily considered it an astonishing thing that while there was no saliva whatever in her mouth, so much sweat was pouring out of her hands that her grip on the rocks was failing. In an ideal world the natural wisdom of the body would distribute its fluids more equitably. She knew there was a ledge three feet below her dangling toes, and Adam had assured her that twelve inches was plenty wide enough for a safe landing, in the unlikely event that she actually fell off this cliff. The trouble was that in her deepest heart Emily no longer trusted Adam's judgment.

She dragged herself up and rested her left forearm on the top of the cliff, keeping the rolled-up towel that was supposed to be her baby held tight in her right arm. Robert Montmorency-Chalmers stood over her, stroking his mustache and leering in the best theatrical tradition. Suddenly he squatted down and put his hand on her arm. That wasn't in the script. Now she was really terrified.

Without moving his lips, he whispered, "Dear lady, are you all right?"

"Why? Why do you ask?"

"Shall I call your husband? Are you going to fall?" His voice sounded warm and caring, not the voice of a murderer.

"No," she said. "Finish the scene." She buried her face in her arm to hide from the camera the feeling of relief that was flooding her being. Chalmers did not intend to kill her. He was a nice man, after all, even though he was an actor.

"Hang on for just a little longer, the scene is almost over. Erno is here," Chalmers murmured. Emily looked up to see the approach of Erno's mud-caked boots. "After we fight I'll pull you right up. It won't take but a minute." A hand appeared on Chalmers's shoulder, Erno's calloused hand with the deeply ingrained grime that he could never seem to remove. He pulled Chalmers back from the cliff's edge. They began the carefully choreographed fight scene, the one they had rehearsed over and over at Chalmers's insistence. Never before had Emily seen them do it from this angle.

As they traded simulated blows Erno's shirt rode up, revealing the bullet-wound scars again. Then all at once, as she clung to the edge of the highest cliff on the Hudson, inches from death, Emily realized the truth. She should have seen it all along. Erno had been shot when he was twelve years old, and not in Finland.

His resemblance to Oskar Heikkinen, the murdered labor agitator, was no accident.

Erno must have been Heikkinen's son, the twelve-year-old who was wounded in Bitter Wash. The grime that would never come out of his hands was the grime of the mines. Of course he would have recognized Duffy in the wig and mustache as the man who killed his father. Of course Big Ed would have confessed to Duffy's murder to protect the son of the woman who had saved his life.

"Ah!" she cried. Stupidly. Erno turned to look at her, and she was not a good enough actress to conceal the fact that she had just realized he was to blame for the murders.

The scuffle moved closer to the cliff. "Erno, what are you doing?" Chalmers said.

Erno's heavy boot came down on Emily's left arm. The pain was terrible. She let go of her hold, shifted the baby, and clung on with her other hand. "Mr. Chalmers, help me! He's trying to kill me!" She had never been so frightened. The tears on her face were real. She almost wished for an actual baby in her arms to comfort her. She hoped the camera was getting all this, because when she died, and it would happen soon, she wanted some trace to be left of her final moments.

Mr. Chalmers struggled valiantly, but he was up against a younger, fitter man. "Easy,

Erno! What are you doing! Aagh!" Then came the sound of a real blow, connecting with some part of Mr. Chalmers, and the thud of a body. Emily waited for Erno to come and kick her off the cliff.

"Aaand . . . cut!" Adam crowed, far away over the brow of the hill.

Yes, he crowed. Why wouldn't he be happy? His last picture was almost finished. Only two more scenes to go, beginning with the scene where Emily's character was rescued from the cliff. Right now, please. "Adam!" she called. "Help me!"

He didn't hear. A commotion was arising at the cliff's edge. With her good arm Emily pulled herself up far enough to see black shoes, the feet of Chief Watson and two of his men. The chief stood over Robert Chalmers, stretched out flat on a pile of rocks.

"I arrest you in the name of the people of New Jersey," Watson was saying, "for the murder of Fay Winningly. Get up and come along."

"He hit his head," Erno said. "We were tussling. It was part of the movie."

"Come on, Mr. Montmorency, get up," the chief said. Mr. Chalmers moaned. The policemen grabbed him under the arms.

Emily called out to him from between Erno's feet: "Help! Chief Watson! I know who the real —" One of Erno's boots came back and hit her a sharp blow on the forehead. The rock at the edge of the cliff slipped out of her grip. She was falling.

Twenty-Four

Adam was well pleased with the way the morning was going. He had managed to stall Chief Watson until the whole scene on the cliff was filmed. Two more brief scenes to go now, the one where Erno's character rescues his young wife and child from the cliff face, and then the final clinch. Audiences liked it when you included a final clinch. It was almost a requirement these days. His stomach rumbled; it was time for a bite to eat, something more substantial than cinnamon buns.

He crossed the street, shuffling his feet through the sweet-smelling yellow leaves, and picked up his rucksack from the steps of the Potts Hotel. Somewhere in that sack was a newspaper-wrapped pastrami sandwich.

It was lucky for Melpomene that the remaining scenes did not require Chalmers. Back on the edge of the cliff Adam saw

Chief Watson's officers lifting him by his arms and carrying him away in the direction of the jailhouse. *Better him than me.* The actor's toes dragged, leaving two scuffed tracks behind him. Drunk again. A day or two in that hellish jail cell would sober the fellow up, probably make a man out of him. When the judge came back from his trip he would surely have enough sense to let the poor sap go. You couldn't condemn a man to death on the strength of a movie still.

A blast of fall air came down the street, stirring the dry leaves into little whirlwinds. Adam almost thought he heard a cry in the distance. He lifted his head and listened for a moment, but heard nothing more. Only the wind. There might even be snow in the air. He blew on his hands and rubbed them together.

The steps of the hotel, warmed by the sun, made a comfortable place to sit and eat his sandwich. Adam took it out of the rucksack, all reeking of garlic and mustard. But as he began to unwrap it, suddenly, there in the paper, looking up at him with a smear of mustard on his nose, was the face of Erno Berg.

Or somebody who looked an awful lot like Erno. And Duffy with his hair and mustache. What was this? A seven-year-old copy of the *New York Journal*. The Bitter Wash riot story. Adam must have wrapped his sandwiches in Emily's archive copy of the *Journal.*

He opened the newspaper and quickly scanned the story. Oskar Heikkinen, killed in the rioting. His twelve-year-old son wounded. The boy would be just about Erno's age. Had Erno actually come from Finland?

Or . . .

Something wasn't right here.

Even before a cause for his alarm had crystallized in his mind Adam was on his feet and crossing the street again, the sandwich forgotten. Something wasn't right here. Murder in the Western mines. A dead detective. Who was Erno Berg, really? Where was Emily? Was she safe? Neither one of them was anywhere in sight. In fact the field by the side of the cliff was quite empty, except for the fire barrel, the bread truck without its horse, the traces lying empty on the ground, and Johnson, bending over his apparatus. He always had to be monkeying with the camera, keeping the alcohol lamp lit, keeping the film supple and free-flowing, keeping the moving parts working the way they should.

"Johnson!"

"Oh, Mr. Weiss. I" — Johnson raised his eyes and focused them somewhere over Adam's left shoulder — "McCoy," he whispered.

Adam turned. A large man was bearing down on them, a bad five-cent cigar protruding from his clenched teeth, its smell going before him, a derby hat on his head, his bulging body encased in a too-tight plaid lounge suit. The man strode toward Johnson, his eye riveted to the camera.

So this was Thomas Edison's principal thug. He was not as tall as Adam, but he was probably tougher. Adam considered the possibility of overcoming him in a fair fight. Or an unfair fight. Whatever it took. The whole morning's shooting was in that camera, footage that could not be retaken without springing Montmorency-Chalmers from jail, which would never happen until the judge came back from Florida. By then it would be too late to save Melpomene. Adam caught Angus Johnson's eye, gestured with his head for him to take the camera and get out of there, and stepped between the detective and the camera.

"So, McCoy. Who's your tailor?" Coarsely woven in mustard and bottle-green, McCoy's suit gave new meaning to the word *loud.*

"You must be Adam Weiss," McCoy said. "They say you murdered Duffy."

"They lie, if they say that," Adam said. "To what do we owe the pleasure?" Why was Johnson still standing there, rooted to the spot? Behind his back Adam flicked his fingers at the cameraman as if to say, go, get lost.

Still Johnson stood immobile.

"I'd like to take a look at your camera," McCoy said. "If you have no objections."

"I have plenty of objections," Adam said. "Take a hike."

"You'd like that, wouldn't you." McCoy put his hand on Adam's shoulder and shoved, attempting to push past him.

"Oh, no, you don't," Adam said. He pushed back.

"Outta my way." McCoy pushed harder.

Adam staggered back a step or two. Furious, he threw a punch at McCoy's midsection. It was like punching a barrel of nails. Coolly McCoy returned the blow, giving Adam one to the jaw that sent him sprawling to the ground. His ears were ringing. Adam shook his head and tried to get up. And still the chowderheaded Johnson stood like a statue. His camera had never looked so precious to Adam, a thing of exquisite beauty, the burnished metal of its fittings glinting in the sunlight, the grainy golden oak of its sides gleaming with flecks of color. Adam's entire future was inside that box, a priceless fortune as long as nobody opened it and exposed it to the light.

"Get out of here, Johnson!" Adam roared, but it was too late. McCoy put out his ham-like hands and yanked the camera away from him.

Wrenching. Twisting. Splintering of wood. With a sharp crack McCoy tore the camera open. "Aw, look at that. It comes apart." Yards and yards of cellulose nitrate curled out and fell on the ground.

A red haze came over everything; Adam struggled to his feet and lunged at McCoy, determined to kill him.

McCoy touched his cigar to the film. A flame shot up. "Now it looks like your film's on fire." He threw the camera at Adam's chest. "Watch out, it's hot."

"You dirty —" Adam sidestepped the burning camera, which fell in the leaves and exploded. He charged McCoy. Braying like the ass he was, the detective danced away from him on the balls of his feet. Graceful for such a stocky fellow. Almost like a prize-fighter.

"Tough on you, Mr. Weiss. I guess I'm a

little slicker than Seamus Duffy. I guess you'll think twice before you go up against Thomas Alva Edison again," McCoy said, and took off running down the road. "I guess you'll think again," he called over his shoulder. "Stupid suckers." Adam could still hear him laughing as he disappeared around the bend and down the road to the ferry.

The leaves had caught fire. Johnson was beating the flames out with his coat. "Let me help you with that," Adam said, and fell to work with his Norfolk jacket. Why not? He was going to be a bum now; he would never need a decent jacket again. "What possessed you to stand there that way? Why didn't you take the camera and go?"

"I had my reasons."

"Oh, you had your reasons. I hope you understand that your reasons have ruined me." Adam ground his foot on the last ember.

"Things could be a lot worse, boss," Johnson said.

"You think so?"

"I do. For instance, this ain't the real camera. It's a decoy. Billy has the real camera in the wagon." A brown hand emerged from a hole in the side of the Butternut Bread wagon and wiggled its fingers.

"You mean we can still —"

"You get the cast together, Mr. Weiss, and we can still finish this picture by the end of the day."

Adam laughed with relief. "Johnson, I could kiss you." But something was still wrong. What was it? He looked around for Emily's old newspaper, the one with the disturbing pictures. He had dropped it; forgotten, it must have blown away. "Where is Mrs. Weiss?"

"Down on that ledge, I think," Johnson said.

"And Erno. Where is he?"

"Said he was going to climb down there and try to give her a hand."

On the narrow ledge far above the rocky shore of the Hudson River, Erno Berg offered Emily his hand, and she took it. "Your hand is hard," was all she could think of to say. She had landed on the ledge when she fell, but landed badly, turning her ankle and coming down hard on her knee. Between the knee and the abrasions on her face and arms she was bleeding in four or five places. None of these wounds seemed to hurt, nor was she bothered anymore by her terror of heights, for her mind and soul had retreated to some cold place deep inside herself, there to wait patiently until things got better. In the meantime, why not take the hand of a murderer? It was all the same.

"My hands are a miner's hands," he said. "A real miner's hands. Not painted." She let him pull her up until she was standing on her good foot. Then he dropped her hand, turned sideways, and pulled his shirt up. "This is a real miner's wound."

"I see."

"No. You don't. You don't see, lady of make-believe. You should have left me alone in the café and let me go back to Finland." He took a few paces away from her, rubbing his hair.

"I'm sorry."

"Big Ed Strawfield told me as soon as we came to Fort Lee. He said I should leave, it wouldn't work, I was no actor."

"He told you to quit the show? Was that what he was saying to you at lunch that day, chattering away in Finnish?"

"That and asking for my mother, who took care of him after he was shot. She's dead now. Cholera."

"I'm sorry for your loss."

"Well. What can you do. When you take the devil aboard, you must row him ashore."

"What does that mean?"

"That means you'll never leave this cliff alive, poor Mrs. Weiss."

"This isn't the way it's supposed to end." Her mother didn't wipe her nose and make her eat her oatmeal for all those years in Eastport so that she could die at the age of twenty-five of a fall from a cliff in Fort Lee, New Jersey.

"The end of the movie, you mean? This is not a movie now. What made you think you could film a story about my father? You and your silly husband. What makes you think you know anything? You make up fluff, and you film it for all the people to watch and they say, yes, that's what life is like. A whole country, a whole world of people drugged with false stories."

"Were you terribly in love with Fay?"

"She was a whore, as false as all the rest of it. She had to die. So do you. I'm finished talking."

He came toward her again, his face still expressionless. She pressed her left shoulder against the wall of the cliff. It gave some support to her broken arm. He took another step. She pressed her torso against the rock as well, keeping her center of gravity as far as possible from the edge of the precipice.

"Don't bother to shout," he said. "I'll simply tell them your foot slipped."

"This is as much talk as I've heard out of your mouth since I've known you," she said.

She pulled her back up straight.

"There was never anything to say." It seemed strange to her that she had ever considered this man to be handsome. His nose was too big. His eyes were too close together. He took another step toward her. She lifted her chin.

His back was too long, his legs were too short, his posture was bad. He had the body of an ape. Emily aligned her own ears with her shoulders, her shoulders with her hips. "You can always say good-bye," she said. Keeping both knees straight, she rose up on the balls of her feet.

"Good-bye, Mrs. Weiss," he said.

She swung her right leg back and then forward as high as she could get it to go. The weeks of exercise paid off.

When her right foot connected with Erno's solar plexus the pain in her damaged ankle was worse than anything she had ever felt. The two of them both screamed at once. Erno had not expected her to kick him. Off balance, he flailed his arms. He grabbed for her, but she cringed away from his hands, and then he went over.

For a long time she stood leaning against the wall of the cliff, panting and sobbing. Eventually some loose pebbles rolled down on her, followed by Adam, scrambling down. "Emily! Are you all right?"

"Not really. Did you get it?"

"Get what?"

"Did you get it on film."

"Sweetheart, you're insane."

"I think I am, yes."

"Where's Erno?"

"At the bottom of the cliff."

He craned his neck out and looked over. "My God, you're right."

"I suppose you're going to scold me now because he can't do the last scene of the movie with me."

"No, I — What happened here?"

"I killed him. I killed the nasty little bugger. He was going to throw me off the cliff, and I gave him a swift kick."

Adam tried to embrace her. It was awkward; she felt damaged. "Is that real blood all over you?" he said.

"Yes, it's real blood, and my own, too, and this is my real arm and it's broken. Also the ankle. I can't support my weight on it."

"Let me help you up the cliff."

"No."

"What?"

"No, Adam. Send the Indians. I want Fred and Billy."

"You don't trust your own husband to get you off this cliff?"

"That's about the size of it. I'm sorry. We'll talk about it when I feel better."

"That's right, sweetheart. We'll talk about it when you feel better. I'll send them. We'll get a rope, maybe rig a bosun's chair or something. You'll be fine."

It took them an hour to pull her up, and another to get the local doctor to see to her injuries. The best light of the day was gone by the time Emily was resting comfortably on a red plush fainting couch in front of the Potts Hotel's parlor fire, her arm set, her chest and ankle taped. Mrs. Potts, clucking like a hen, brought her a stiff drink of her favorite tipple. Emily downed the glass of Fernet-Branca most gratefully. Bitter and nasty going down, it spread warmth and comfort throughout her being like an internal mustard plaster.

Now she felt almost ready to plumb the deeper secrets of Seamus Duffy's memoirs. "Mrs. Potts, can I ask you to bring me the manila envelope I left on the kitchen table?"

"You mean that big envelope addressed to Mr. Weiss? The one our stable hand found in the yard in a mud puddle?"

"Yes."

"Mr. Bruns threw it in the kitchen stove as soon as your back was turned."

"What!" Emily sprang to her feet and was immediately sorry. The pain in her ankle was dreadful.

"Sit down, child," Mrs. Potts said. "Too late to do anything about it now, it's gone. Made an awful mess, too, flaming crumbs of paper flying all over my kitchen. You'd think a man with as much sophistication as Mr. Bruns claims to have would know how to put the lid back on a kitchen stove."

"I'll kill him. Where is he?"

"He took the first trolley out of Fort Lee as soon as he saw that envelope burn up. Now you just sit there and rest," Mrs. Potts said. "I have to get back to my work."

"If I ever see him again I'll kill him," Emily muttered.

"Who?" Adam was indulging in his new habit of coming through doors without making any noise.

"Holbert Bruns. I've been keeping something from you. He's not really an actor, Adam."

"I thought his rushes looked excellent. How are you feeling?"

"Unwell."

"You're looking pretty spry, though. You could even come outside and do just one more thing for me before the sun goes down."

"What?"

"That last scene, where you and the baby are rescued from the cliff. I was just talking to Johnson. The camera is still set up for the shot. I know Erno can't be in it now, but couldn't we — ? Wait a minute. I've got it. For the rescue scene, you can come out with me right now, while we still have enough light to film the scene, and hang out over the cliff. Slowly, slowly you pull yourself up over the edge. You're saved! You and the baby. Then for the final clinch we'll use one of the Indians, dress him in a shirt like Erno's, put a wig on him, powder his hands, and —"

"Adam, my arm is broken."

"But surely that shouldn't —"

"My ribs are probably broken, too. My ankle is sprained. I'm terrified of heights. Nothing in heaven or on earth could induce me to go back out on that cliff."

He blinked, frowned, and searched her face, incredulous. "Emily, sweetheart, this is important. To me. To us." Adam was not used to being balked of his will, least of all by Emily.

She returned his gaze steadily. "No, Adam. I can't do it, you see."

"I wonder whether you realize what your refusal will mean for Melpomene Moving

Picture Studios." He rubbed his head with both hands, anger giving way to distraction. "Ruin, is what. Nothing less than complete ruin. Howie Kazanow will get every penny I've ever worked for. To think that I should be stabbed in the back by my own wife."

Emily didn't know whether to laugh at him or burst out crying. Either way it would make her chest hurt. "Adam. Look at me."

He stopped pacing and tearing his hair and looked at her.

"My bones are broken," she said. "Everything hurts. I'm exhausted. I gave Melpomene all I had. There isn't any more."

Then, finally, she could see him noticing her, his wife, tired and in pain. He loved her after all. He was sorry for the way he had treated her.

"I haven't been very good to you lately, have I?" he said.

"No."

"Can you forgive me?" Kneeling before her, he put his head in her lap and hugged her legs. How could she not forgive him?

"Of course I can." She petted his hair with her good hand. His head was heavy and warm and smelled of brilliantine.

"We're going to have some very hard times now," he mumbled into her leg. "It's my fault. I'm so sorry, Emily."

"We'll get through it," she said. "It'll be all right."

He sprang up and began to pace the room again. "If only we had another actress who could stunt for you."

"Maybe you could telephone one of the agencies in the city."

"By the time they sent somebody it would be too dark."

Emily sighed and stared into the fire. In the leaping flames she saw the wreck of all their hopes, herself compelled to go back on the stage, Adam forced to degrade himself making sandwiches at Horn and Hardart, his manhood shriveling away day by day. Poverty and destitution.

Then the storm door banged, and a slim figure came tripping into the hotel parlor. As the young woman approached her Emily saw that it was none other than the former Leola Dietz, now known as Gwendolyn Gwynne, with her mass of golden hair.

"Mrs. Weiss! They told me I could find you in here. The Actophone studio burned to the ground, and we're all out of work now. Do you think you might have any parts for me?"

"Ah, Miss Gwynne," Emily said. "How happy I am to see you. I believe we do have something. How's your head for heights?"

AUTHOR'S NOTE

What is real? What is not?

For more than a decade there really was a thriving moving picture industry in Fort Lee, New Jersey. Fort Lee was quite a different town before the George Washington Bridge was built, offering a pleasing variety of scenery and a home for the glass-roofed studios of the time. Thomas Edison's Motion Picture Patents Company was a serious threat to independent filmmakers. Film scholar Richard Koszarski has written a number of books on the subject of early moviemaking, the most entertaining of which is *Fort Lee: The Film Town,* a collection of primary sources including actual reports written by Thomas Edison's Trust detectives.

Konstantin Sergeyevich Stanislavsky's Moscow Art Theater was in full flower in the early part of the twentieth century. Every now and then a real method actor would come to America and get into the movies, long before Lee Strasberg, Brando, and the rest.

There was no such thing as the Bitter Wash massacre, although there could have been. I based the incident on many other labor-management confrontations that took place in the late nineteenth and early twentieth century, pitched battles in many cases: the Haymarket riot, the Pullman strike, the Homestead rebellion, the troubles in Coeur d'Alene, Butte, and Cripple Creek, the Ludlow massacre. In those days the Pinkertons detectives (as well as other agencies, and sometimes the state militia) acted as a police force for rent to the mine and mill owners. Their job was to destroy the unions by any means necessary, while the role of the more radical unions, as they sometimes saw it, was to seize control of the wealth of which they saw themselves as the creators. Bloody confrontations between the two sides continued right up into the Franklin D. Roosevelt administration.

There was a governor, Frank Steunenberg, who was foully murdered by Harry Orchard in 1905. The incident was treated in great depth by J. Anthony Lukas in his book *Big Trouble,* the definitive picture of the turn-of-the-century American labor scene.

There was never a Big Ed Strawfield, for I made him up and patterned him after Big Bill Haywood. While Mr. Haywood was quite the boy, he never had a Russian movie star for a lover, that I'm aware of.

— Lambertville, New Jersey, 2010

ABOUT THE AUTHOR

Irene Fleming lives in Lambertville, New Jersey. Writing as Kate Gallison, she is the author of eight previous crime novels.

We hope you have enjoyed this Large Print book. Other Thorndike, Wheeler, Kennebec, and Chivers Press Large Print books are available at your library or directly from the publishers.

For information about current and upcoming titles, please call or write, without obligation, to:

Publisher
Thorndike Press
295 Kennedy Memorial Drive
Waterville, ME 04901
Tel. (800) 223-1244

or visit our Web site at:

http://gale.cengage.com/thorndike

OR

Chivers Large Print
published by AudioGO Ltd
St James House, The Square
Lower Bristol Road
Bath BA2 3BH
England
Tel. +44(0) 800 136919
email: info@audiogo.co.uk
www.audiogo.co.uk

All our Large Print titles are designed for easy reading, and all our books are made to last.